Edna Hong

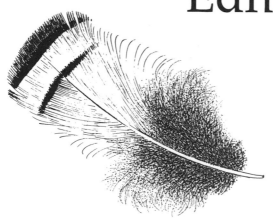

ILLUSTRATIONS BY KAREN FOGET

PULU DID IT!

How a Wild Partridge
Became a Family Pet

A-R EDITIONS, INC. • MADISON, WISCONSIN

Library of Congress Cataloging in Publication Data

Hong, Edna Hatlestad, 1913–
Pulu did it!: How a wild partridge became a family pet / by Edna Hong ;
drawings by Karen Foget
p. cm.
Summary: A family's partridge proves an enchanting pet and they take
Pulu everywhere, though its sexual identity seems to be a mystery.
ISBN 0-89579-233-8
1. Chukar partridge—Fiction. [1. Chukar partridge—Fiction.
2. Partridges—Fiction.] I. Foget, Karen, ill. II. Title.
PS3515.04974P8 1989
813'.54—dc19
[Fic]
88-34149
CIP

A-R Editions, Inc.
801 Deming Way
Madison, Wisconsin 53717 (608) 836-9000

10   9   8   7   6   5   4   3   2   1

Contents

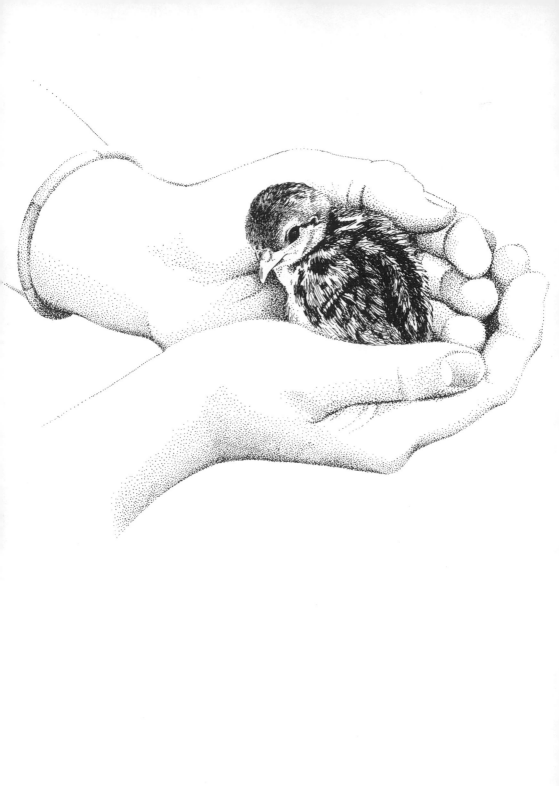

Enter Pulu

Very likely Pulu would never have become a member of the Malecha household if it had not been for the mother's allergies. Cats and dogs had been tried as pets several times, but always with the same result—Alison's irritated eyes, nose, throat, and temper. By the age of ten, the twins, Michael and Melanie, were more or less reconciled to having no pets, but they continued to explore options for non-allergenic pets and to quarrel about them.

"Michael wants a snake!" wailed Melanie, one day early in May. "A nasty slimy snake! If you let him bring a snake into this house I'm going to go live with Bestemor and Grandpa!"

"Snakes are not nasty and slimy!" snapped Michael, his greenish-blue eyes flashing fire, his freckles blazing, and his carroty hair almost standing on end. "And a boa constrictor is

1

harmless! Tom Dawson has one in a cage in his basement."

"Boa constrictors can grow to be ten feet long," said Philip, the father, doubtfully.

"Boa constrictors don't eat hamburger or anything dead," added Alison quietly. "What does Tom feed his snake?"

"His grandpa owns a hatchery and he goes there and gets live chicks," answered Michael uncomfortably.

"And you watch the snake swallow those darling little chicks alive?" squealed Melanie, her gypsy brown eyes (obviously they are not identical twins) wide with horror. She tugged at a strand of her long black hair, as she always did when she was most upset with Michael.

A few days later . . .

"Now he wants a tarantula! A big ugly black spider that makes you sick even if it doesn't make you die!"

Michael was dissuaded from the tarantula when he learned that it, too, insisted on a diet of live things and that his weekly allowance would have to be spent on live beetles for his pet.

"Why does Michael want such a gross pet as a boa constrictor or a tarantula?" asked Melanie.

"Because they're interesting!" snapped Michael. "You just want dumb pets like goldfish and baby chicks."

"Baby chicks are cute."

"Baby chicks grow up to be dull fat old hens."

"And cute human babies grow up to be scrappy ten-year-olds!" laughed Philip. "Why don't you two simmer down and we'll all try to talk calmly about this. Let's start with something we can all agree on. Premise one, to wit."

"To what?" asked the twins.

"Your father is talking college jargon again."

"Knock it off, Dad!"

"OK, Son. Point one. Your mother and I agree with you that our family should have a pet, a non-allergenic pet. But we

2

think it should be a pet with which we can all bond and that will bond with us."

Michael: "What does 'bond' mean? I thought it had something to do with money."

Philip: "It means to develop a fond relation with some other creature that is capable of being fond of you. I can't imagine bonding with a tarantula."

Michael: "Or with a girl."

Philip: "Hey, now! Have you forgotten one of the ten Malecha family commandments? 'Thou shalt not put anyone down.' Argue with, yes, but not put down."

Michael: "I was just teasing."

"I was bonded with Goosey Gander, but he didn't bond with me," mourned Melanie.

"I didn't bond with Goosey Gander," said Michael matter-of-factly. "He got too big and fat and dull. I didn't miss him a bit when we ate him for Thanksgiving."

"Geese have been domesticated for centuries," said Philip. "A pair of geese very likely tagged behind Adam and Eve when they were banished from Paradise. I suspect Goosey Gander was so civilized and so bonded with us two-legged creatures without feathers that he didn't even rise up to his full gander height, beat his wings, and respond with a cry of longing when the wild geese flew overhead. At least I never saw him trying to raise his big hulk to join his wild relatives."

"I wonder," said Alison suddenly, "if a really wild bird would bond with human beings. I mean a bird that has no history of domestication. A bird that still belongs to a wild and timid clan."

"You just gave me a wild idea!" said Philip—and would not tell them what it was.

Enter Pulu!

Not a quail, not a grouse, not a pheasant. On their almost

3

every Sunday hikes along the twenty miles of trails in the University of Wisconsin-Madison Arboretum, the Malechas had become rather well acquainted with the family that included those birds.

Not a gray partridge, whose "bobwhite" call they had heard many a time on the trail that crossed the edge of Wingra Marsh and skirted Ho-Nee-Um Pond.

"It's a chukar partridge," said Philip, handing a shoe box to Alison when he arrived home from the university later than usual the next day. "I found us a bird that 'belongs to a wild and timid clan,' quoting your mother, Kids. I went to the Department of Wildlife Ecology and saw Perry, the fellow I met and ran with at the Stoughton Marathon last summer. I remembered that he works there. Well, it just so happens—another strange case of serendipity in our family—that they had a brood of chukar partridge chicks hatch this morning, and Perry let me have one."

Melanie stopped practicing her piano lesson and Michael stopped setting the dining room table.

"A *what* partridge?" asked Michael, eyeing the box eagerly.

"A chukar partridge. It's a native of the slopes of the Himalaya Mountains. Know where they are, Mike?"

"The Himalayas are a terrifically high mountain range between Tibet and India," Michael answered promptly. "I had to report on them yesterday. They've got the highest mountain in the world, Mt. Everest."

"Correct! Go to the head of the class! That's where this chukar partridge chick's ancestors lived. Perry says that the chukar partridge was introduced rather recently as a game bird into forty-two states of the United States and six Canadian provinces, but it survived only in British Columbia and ten western states. It didn't take to Wisconsin or Minnesota. Seems to prefer steep mountain sides, sagebrush, and sun-dried grass. Perry

4

says it's a very favorite game bird for hunters because it's so smart and tough. Climbs like a mountain goat and blasts off like a jet. But it doesn't scare easily. A covey of a hundred chukars can hide from hunters tramping all over and around them and not stir a feather or make a sound. The hunters go back to camp and report no chukars in sight."

"Golly, Dad, we don't want a lecture!" scolded Michael. "We want to see this bird!"

Melanie tugged impatiently at Alison's arm. "Mom, why don't you open the box?"

Alison held the box with both hands against her heart.

"I have such a strange feeling! I remember feeling like this when your father gave me my engagement ring. I could hardly make myself open the jewelry box because I felt that what was inside was going to be so precious that I couldn't bear it. Will you open it for me, Melanie and Michael?"

Almost instinctively the four of them moved to the solid wall of window facing the eastern half of the arboretum and knelt before their own interior mini-arboretum in tubs and half-barrels set upon slate-blue pebbles from the shores of Lake Superior and interspersed with pieces of driftwood and peregrine rocks they had found on their camping trips. They knelt in a half-circle in front of a pottery-tubbed mugho pine. Alison set the box on the slate floor. Carrot head and dark head bowed over it, and four hands reached almost shyly and timidly to lift the cover of the shoe box.

Up from the nest of Philip's Pendleton virgin wool cap leaped—almost as if it were a jack-in-the-box—a tiny ball of fluffy down. It perched on toothpick legs on the rim of the box and promptly began to chirp, then leaped to the floor and disappeared within the mini-arboretum. The startled four rose to their feet and followed the partridge's scampering around the plant containers.

5

"Little did we know when we built this house that we were building it for a native of the Himalayas," chuckled Philip.

Michael finally captured the partridge chick behind the dwarf spruce. He cupped it tenderly in his hands.

"You little rascal, you!"

Then, because the chick was so preposterously tiny (and to its partridge eye, they imagined, they were so outrageously monstrous), they all lay down on the floor, forming a circle around it.

"We must look like the Himalaya mountain range to him," laughed Alison.

"Peep! Peep!" called Philip. "Come, you wild little migrant! Come climb the slopes and cliffs of Mt. Philip!"

To their delight the partridge chick leaped on Philip's foot, ran the full length of his body, and snuggled contentedly under his jutting chin.

"Shh!" whispered Philip. "I think he's bonding!"

"He isn't the *only* one bonding," said Michael.

"How do you know it's a HE?" challenged Melanie. "And may I hold HER, please?"

The chick did not seem to mind being cuddled by all four of them in turn.

"I have a sudden curiosity about what the adult chukar partridge looks like," said Philip, scrambling to his feet. "I wonder if the Audubon Society bird book has a picture of it."

It did.

"He's beautiful!" exclaimed Philip. "Red-orange legs and bill. Looks a little bigger than the partridge and is predominantly—I don't know what to say! I see gray and brown and buff and tan and even chestnut in his overall color. What makes him so striking are the black bars on his flanks—almost like black ribs. And there's a wide black band that seems to go right though his eyes and circles a cream-colored bib. His eyes are like black pearls. I don't see how anyone could make a mistake identifying a chukar partridge. Little one, you are going to grow up to be a right handsome male!"

"There you go again, Daddy!" scolded Melanie. "HE—HE—MALE—MALE! How do you know that this bird is a male?"

"Well, Melanie, I guess you are right. We won't know for sure until he—"

"SHE!"

"Until he or she grows a comb or doesn't grow a comb. Meanwhile we can't just call this lovely chick 'it.' Does anyone have a good name for him or her?"

"Patrick!" cried Michael.

"Patty!" cried Melanie, who now held the partridge chick cuddled against her cheek. "Patty Partridge!"

"Well, well, another Malecha twin cul-de-sac. No way out but to call this bird after me!"

"Philip?" the other three chorused.

Michael: "You're kidding, Dad!!"

Philip: "We'll call him Pip, which is a shortened form of Philip. If you don't believe me, see the index of masculine names in the Random House dictionary. If and when Pip turns out to be a female, we'll call her Pippa. After Browning's Pippa in *Pippa Passes*.

"The year's at the spring
And day's at the morn;
Morning's at seven;
The hillside's dew-pearled;
The lark's on the wing;
The snail's on the thorn:
God's in his heaven—
All's right with the world!"

7

Michael: "Now you're talking college again. But Pip's a good name. Let's call him Pip."

Alison: "Until otherwise informed, Melanie and I will call her Pippa."

Philip: "So! Now we're in a Malecha husband-wife cul-de-sac! Let me think! Aha! I have it! I just finished reading a novel called *The Journeyer* that recreates the journey Marco Polo made in the thirteenth century. There's a chapter in it called 'The Roof of the World,' meaning Tibet. There might be some good names in it we could all agree on. Here, Nameless One, I'm going to let you scamper around in our mini-arboretum while we find a name for you."

Philip quickly fetched Gary Jenning's novel from his study and skimmed through the pages.

"Here's a Kalash dance Marco Polo observed on the roof of the world. It was called Kikli."

"Kikli! That sounds good to me," said Alison.

"It sounds too girly," muttered Michael.

"Hey, now!" cried Philip in excitement. "Marco Polo saw the chukar partridge! At a place called Bunzai Gumbad he saw many red-legged partridges with clipped wings. The children played hide-and-seek with them. Marco Polo says that they were kept for either pets or pest killers. And—hey, get this, you Malecha women! The Kalash women cut off the red legs of the partridges that were slaughtered to go into the pot, burned the legs to a fine ash. It turned out to be a purple powder that they used as a cosmetic to beautify their eyes!"

"And we think purple-shadowing our eyes is so modern!" said Alison.

Philip, swiftly turning pages, let out a whoop.

"Here's a name that ought to satisfy all of us! Pulu! It's the name for a rounded knot of willow wood the natives hit with heavy sticks toward two goals. Sounds something like our field hockey."

8

"Pulu! Pulu!"

The twins repeated the name and nodded their heads.

"When your father and I were discussing names for you two, Melanie and Michael, we tested each name to see if it was an easy name to call. Pulu is a marvelous calling name."

Alison threw back her head and called, "PU-U-U-U-U-U-LU!"

"It's a much better calling name than Osmond or Harold or William. Furthermore, it's a name that's neither male nor female. And it comes from the roof of the world where this chukar chick's ancestors lived and were seen and described by Marco Polo. How about it? Is the name Pulu?"

"Here, Pulu, Pulu," called Melanie.

The downy little ball of fluff came running from behind the sago palm and ran up Melanie's leg.

"I think Pulu is bonded," whispered Melanie, genuinely awestruck.

"I think Pulu is hungry," said Alison.

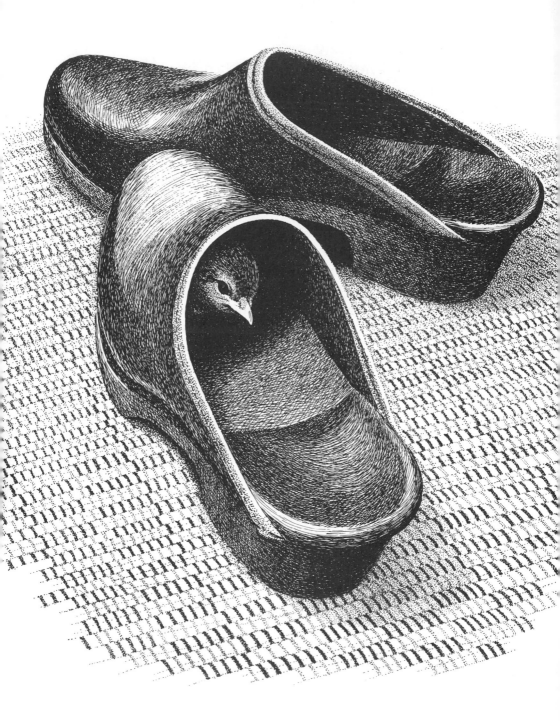

A Place for Pulu

They scattered the pelletized duck food Perry had sent along with the chick in front of the fireplace on the north wall. Pulu exhibited no interest whatever.

"Pulu seems to prefer exploring his new home to eating," said Philip.

"Do you suppose she doesn't like duck food?" wondered Alison.

The twins took turns running to the kitchen for various and sundry foods that might be more tempting. Oatmeal (the old-fashioned kind), crushed Cheerios, and crumbled Shredded Wheat were all spurned. Even crumbs of Oakhouse Bakery's homemade, homeground wheat bread with no additives roused no interest.

"Do you suppose mother partridges feed their babies the

way the robins in our maple tree feed their young? Do you suppose Pulu will make it without his mother?" worried Michael.

"Fortunately, Pulu belongs to the order of pecking birds and not the order of gaping birds. I'll go call Perry and tell him Pulu won't eat his duck food and find out what we should do."

While Philip was gone, Alison compared Pulu to the just-hatched pigeon she had observed in the rain gutter outside the window of the sixth floor of the office building where she had worked as a secretary before the twins had been born.

"I had always thought that all baby birds were adorable. I could never accept Thomas Huxley's definition of a bird as a glorified reptile, but when I saw that pigeon chick I almost believed Huxley was right. I had never seen anything so ugly. It didn't have a bit of fuzz on its body. All its innards were visible under its thin pinkish-purplish skin. At the end of its scrawny neck was a huge gaping beak. Oh, Pulu, you restore my faith in the adorableness of baby birds!"

Alison scooped the chick up in her hands.

"Look!" she cried, "she's poking her head through the circle of my thumb and forefinger! Oh, Pulu, you *are* adorable!"

Alison cuddled Pulu to her cheek.

"Mom?"

Melanie was tugging at a strand of her hair and looking worried.

"Yes, Melanie?"

"Is your nose itching?"

"Are you feeling any sneezes coming?" asked Michael, looking just as worried.

"Oh, you darlings!" laughed Alison. "You're afraid I'm going to be allergic to Pulu! Don't worry! I'm no more allergic to feathered friends than I am to my family. Wouldn't it be horrible if I were allergic to you two and to your daddy?"

"If ever you are," said Philip, returning from his telephoning, "we'll build a big cage for you out of clear plastic and keep you as a pet. Our unpettable pet."

"What about Pulu?" chorused the twins, ignoring their father's silliness as they were in the habit of doing.

"Perry says not to worry. Pulu is gallinacious. The word comes from the Latin word *gallina* for hen, which means that Pulu belongs to the same order as the chicken."

Alison: "Goodness gracious! Gallinacious! Well, at least Pulu isn't pugnacious—or fallacious—or salacious!"

Michael: "Now *you* are being silly, Mom!"

Philip: "What a burden—two silly parents!"

Melanie: "When are you going to tell us what to feed Pulu?"

Michael: "Without the biology lecture, Dad."

Philip: "Ah, but the biology of Pulu is very important. Being gallinacious, he feeds on the yoke of his egg. It's the white of the egg that makes the chick, and the yoke provides its rations for the first day or so. Perry says that he will be hungry tomorrow morning. Tomorrow, Pulu, you will be voracious as well as gallinacious."

Alison: "So that's what Pulu is running on—the yoke of her egg! It must be a peppy pabulum. Did you ever see a bird so full of running?"

Melanie: "Have you forgotten the baby sandpiper we saw in Wingra Park, Mom? It never stopped running, and its mother was nearly crazy trying to keep up with it."

Michael: "What about tonight? Where is Pulu going to sleep? Can he sleep in my room?"

Philip: "We have to do something about that, and pretty quickly, too. Perry says that at the Wild Game Farm they set the thermostat at 95° for baby chicks for the first ten days and 80° for the next twenty."

"Ninety-five degrees!" exclaimed Michael. He ran to the

13

thermostat. "It's set at 68°. Shall I push it up to 95°?"

"And drive us out of the house? Move outdoors and let Pulu have the house? No, thanks!" said Philip emphatically. "We'll have to make a temporary house for Pulu. Perry says a sturdy, roomy cardboard box with the flaps closed and a light bulb hanging from the top will do. He emphasized having a rough bath towel on the bottom so that his toes develop properly."

For the time being, a Jack Daniels carton served as a box too high for Pulu to jump out of. They proceeded to make it habitable and homey for a motherless partridge chick. Alison rummaged in the cedar chest for her angora tam and fitted it loosely over the top of a six-inch Danish pepper mill.

"That's a substitute for her mother's wings."

Philip suspended a socketed 40-watt light bulb on an electric cord through the closed flaps of the box.

"The light bulb will help Pulu think he's nestling under his mother's warm wings."

"Golly, Dad!" objected Michael. "Would *you* like to sleep under an electric light bulb all night?"

"Would you rather be warm or dark?"

"When I go to sleep I want to be warm *and* dark."

"If you can't have both?"

"Well, warm, I guess."

They finally decided that an electric heating pad set at its lowest and placed under the towel would keep the box warm enough. Philip removed the light bulb. They inserted a thermometer in the box, set the dial on high, and raised the temperature to 95° before they lowered the dial to low.

"Now I think Pulu should go to bed. After all, she's a newborn infant."

"Aw, Mom! He's too perky yet to go to bed."

14

"Maybe he's running frantically to keep warm. Your mother is right," said Philip.

Pulu seemed grateful to be placed in the semi-dark box and cuddled under the angora tam as if it were his mother's wing. A few sleepy contented peeps and then silence.

"Thank goodness!" sighed Melanie. "I don't think I could eat or sleep if Pulu hadn't liked her box."

"Perhaps your dad and I should parent Pulu the first night of her life with us. As a matter of fact, the very first night of her life!" said Alison. When she saw Michael's mouth opening to make his claim, she added hastily, "Maybe tomorrow night. We'll all take turns at parenting Pulu! Right?"

The Malecha household, including its newest member, slept peacefully all night long. The real night, that is, not the metaphorical night. When the morning stars, Mercury and Venus, began to fade at 5:30 A.M. and the sun arose, Pulu announced from his box that it was time for all living, breathing creatures to be up and doing. Philip looked at his digital watch, groaned, turned over, and pulled the cambric cotton down comforter over his head. But the twins, strangely enough, heard Pulu's morning call to arise and seize the day and padded into the bedroom, as wide awake and alert as Pulu. They removed the throw rug from the top of the box, opened the flaps, lifted Pulu out, and deposited him on the queen-size bed. Pulu peep-peeped his delight to be free and skirred up and down and over the rumpled slopes of the down comforter.

"I wonder if he knows that it's filled with 'a superior blend of hand-selected white goose and duck down,' " muttered Philip, who was trying to forget what his birthday gift to Alison had cost.

Pulu beelined to the hidden source of the voice, tunneled in, and peeped joyously. Philip sat bolt upright.

15

"Hey, this little tike already knows how to play hide-and-seek. Remember Marco Polo? He reported that the kids at Bunzai Gumbad played hide-and-seek with the red-legged partridges."

"Maybe she's not playing but crying for her breakfast," said Alison. All five of them vacated the bedroom and went to the living room, where yesterday's hodgepodge of pelletized duck food, oatmeal, Cheerios, Shredded Wheat, and bread crumbs still lay on the fireplace hearth. But Pulu once again ignored the food and disappeared behind the plants in the mini-arboretum.

"Golly, he's still living on egg yolk!" marveled Michael.

But Alison, obeying a sudden hunch as to what a mother chukar partridge might do, tapped her finger on the hearth. Pulu raced out from behind the sago palm to the tapping sound and began to pick hungrily but daintily at the food.

"What a relief!" sighed Philip.

Lying on their sides, heads on arms akimbo, they flanked Pulu and watched him eat. Quite soon replete, the chukar chick stood still and looked at each one of them.

"I wonder what she's thinking," said Melanie.

"I think he's thinking that we four are the greatest chukar partridges in the chukar partridge world," said Philip.

"Do you really believe Pulu thinks she's one of us?" asked Melanie.

"I think he thinks we are one of him."

Michael combed his fingers through his carroty hair.

"Hey!" he cried in mock alarm, "my hair is turning to feathers!"

"If it really does," chuckled Philip, "you will look more like a redheaded woodpecker than a chukar partridge."

Pulu darted to a pool of sunlight already beginning to be warm.

16

"Do we have to put her back in the box?" asked Melanie.

Philip: "For a few days, perhaps—to be sure that his body temperature stays where it should be. But I can't imagine Mother Chukar coddling her brood on those Himalayan slopes! Maybe now is the time to decide whether we make a kind of indoor pen for Pulu or give him the freedom of the whole house."

"Remember that what goes in comes out again, Kids," said Alison. "We've got to face that a bird is a feathered alimentary canal that swallows at one end and ejects at the other."

"Can we train Pulu to use a litter box?" wondered Melanie.

"I doubt it, Melanie. We'll just have to see what kind of toilet habits Pulu has."

At that very moment Pulu emerged from behind a piece of driftwood and deposited a tiny hard pellet on the hearth.

"There's our answer!" laughed Alison. "A neat little snippet that will vacuum up like a fleck of dust. I won't mind that—as long as Pulu doesn't drop them into the soup."

So it was decided then and there that Pulu would be granted the freedom of the house when he graduated from the box.

"But the ladies in my book club will be horrified when they meet here next month and find out that we allow a wild bird the freedom of the house. I'll have to tell them that Annie Dillard, whom they all admire, gives spiders the freedom of her house, tolerates spider webs, and even leaves a bath towel draped over the bathtub so that spiders trapped in the tub can use its rough surface for an exit ramp."

"Bully for Annie Dillard!" said Michael, who was reluctant to dust away cobwebs for reasons other than tenderness toward living creatures.

"Speaking of spiders," said Philip at the dinner table a few days later, "I took Pulu out on the porch today and let him

17

scamper around out there because the sun was so warm. He chased his first spider. Don't tell Annie Dillard, but it looks as if we will have a spiderless house. What a bright little fellow! I'm convinced a chukar partridge is born from the egg with a fully developed digestive system, a wide-awake brain, and lively legs as well as a coat of downy tan-brown feathers."

"By the way, Kids," Philip continued, "you probably will approve that I dismissed someone's idea of calling our bird Marco Pulu."

"Aw, Dad!" groaned the twins.

Gradually Pulu's short tastes of freedom became too sweet for him to put up with life in a box. He began hiding from them when he suspected that his liberty leave was over. Under the beds, in the toes of Alison's clogs, in Michael's winter boots.

By this time they were beginning to recognize Pulu's calls.

"I'm lost! I'm lost!"

"Where are you? You're too far away!"

"I'm lonesome! Come here at once!"

"Take me out of this wretched box!"

"I'm hungry! Feed me!"

But Pulu in hiding was utterly silent.

Food, Feathers—Flight!

 It was Philip's turn to make breakfasts the first week in June. When the sleepy family came to the table one morning they found five, not four, settings of their best pottery plates. In the center of the table was a bowl of lilacs so freshly picked that a few jewels of dew still clung to the leaves. Alison's eyebrows elevated.

"What are we celebrating? And who is the mystery guest?"

"We are celebrating the fact that at 9:00 P.M. today the moon is at apogee."

"Oh, no, we're not!" laughed Alison, throwing her arms around his neck. "We're celebrating the fact that Philip Prochazka Malecha just found a new word for his book, *An Exaltation of Words*. OK, philologist, what does 'apogee' mean?"

"It's the point at which the moon and the earth are farthest apart. Two hundred fifty-two thousand, six hundred twenty-eight miles. The point of its shortest distance is called perigee. But that's not what we are really celebrating. What we are really celebrating is our mystery guest, whom I shall now usher in. No, you fetch him, Michael. Fetch him in the box, and I'll fix his plate."

"Pulu?" they chorused.

"Pulu, of course! We are celebrating Pulu's graduation from the box. Today is the day we stop mollycoddling one of the toughest birds in the world. He and we are going to feast on the first strawberries from our garden, Oscar Mayer pork sausage, and Oakhouse Bakery's pumpkin muffins."

Pulu, peeping with joy, was lifted from the box and passed from hand to hand.

"You are still just a little ball of down, Pulu," crooned Alison. Then, lightly touching the tan-brown fluff and parting it, she cried with excitement.

"Look! Her feathers are beginning to grow under this fluff and are pushing it out!"

As was proper for an honored guest, Pulu was served first. Philip, with a white napkin draped over his left wrist, carried Pulu's plate in and set it between Melanie and Michael with a flourish.

" 'Vaers'go, Pulu!' as Bestemor so nicely says, or 'Prosin te jse,' as Babička always says."

Pulu stood on his toothpick legs on the rim of the plate and eyed the food with bright beadlike eyes.

"Please notice that Pulu does not act greedy," said Alison, who, thank goodness, was not often guilty of making otherwise pleasant occasions teacherly. In fact, she had raised the twins on Sesyle Joslin's hilarious two volumes on "proper conduct for all occasions": *What Do You Say, Dear?* and *What Do You Do, Dear?*

22

"I wonder what she'll peck at first," said Melanie.

"I apologize, Sir," said Philip, "for not being able to serve you a breakfast of wild rose hips and box-elder bug omelet. This is the best our kitchen can do."

But Pulu had already proved that he was omnivorous and not too, too fastidious about what he ate. He was only taking his time to decide between the delectables. The plump red-red strawberry captured his will first, but after he had pecked at the cut-up bits of pork sausage he ate every piece of that before wiping his bill daintily and moving to the pumpkin muffin.

Pulu was so couth and delicate in his dining that they decided then and there to invite him to dine with them often, but not always. They soon learned to know his most favorite foods. Scrambled eggs with Oscar Mayer luncheon meat. Steak cut into small pieces. Dandelion greens and watercress.

As for his most unfavorite food, they discovered what that was a week later when Bestemor and Grandpa Mason came for dinner. It was supposed to have been a picnic in the back yard, but mosquitoes and the threat of an evening thunderstorm turned the picnic into an indoor meal. Or a feast! Bestemor provided the fried chicken for which she was famous in her church and neighborhood. Chicken fried crisply brown on the outside, tender as a ripe peach on the inside. Grandpa Mason, who had not blinked an eye at having a wild bird sit at the table with him, cut a chicken breast into small pieces and put it on Pulu's plate. Pulu eyed it thoughtfully, touched a piece with his bill, and then pushed it away. He absolutely refused to eat it and peeped loudly for something else to be put on his plate.

"Maybe Pulu is a vegetarian," said Bestemor. "Seems as if every other young thing is that nowadays."

Michael: "No, Bestemor. Pulu is not a vegetarian. He's crazy about steak and sausage and bacon. He's really acting awfully funny about your chicken!"

23

Melanie: "She doesn't know what she's missing, Bestemor! No one makes chicken as good as you do."

Philip: "An incredible thought is sneaking into my brain! If it's true, then before our eyes at this table tonight Pulu is demonstrating one of the most noble instincts animating living creatures. The instinct to be true to creatures of the same kind. Pulu is refusing to eat the meat of his feathered relatives! It's absolutely uncanny!"

Michael: "I'll bet Pulu would eat chicken if he was starving! Even humans do that. I saw a movie on TV about some starving people who would have died if they hadn't eaten the flesh of those who had just died of starvation."

"Please, Michael!" pleaded Bestemor, visibly distressed by the turn of the table conversation.

A sharp crack of thunder assured them of the wisdom of their decision to eat indoors. When the power had been knocked out for an hour they lit candles and lingered long at the table. To Grandpa's delight, Pulu sat on his shoulder after pecking curiously at his hearing aid and snuggled close to his ear.

"Look at that flash of lightning!" cried Melanie.

"Can't look! Don't dare turn my head!" chuckled Grandpa.

Philip: "I'm wondering if Pulu tastes. After all, poultry don't chew their food. It goes from the esophagus right into the crop."

Michael: "Crop? Is that the same as the gizzard? Who got the gizzards tonight? It was *my* turn to have the gizzards!"

Bestemor: "I'm so sorry, Michael! I cooked the gizzards and hearts and chopped them up. I'm going to cream them tomorrow and have them on toast."

Grandpa: "Speaking of gizzards or a bird's crop, that reminds me of something in a book I was reading just today. It's that *Old Rails and Fence Corners* you gave me for Christmas, Alison. It's all about the old times. One of the stories is told by a

24

ninety-five-year-old man about a visit to his sister at the Lac qui Parle Presbyterian mission on the Minnesota River way back in 1841. The old man remembered a patch of wheat the missionaries were growing way out there on the western prairie. Where do you suppose they got the seed for the wheat? You'll never guess so I'll have to tell you. In the crop of a trumpeter swan! The swan had flown down the river from the settlement up the Red River, where wheat had been grown for some time. The missionaries called the patch of wheat Red River Wheat."

Philip: "That reminds *me*, Grandpa, that I had better buy some ground-up limestone for Pulu. After all, he isn't running on stony foothills or pebble-strewn canyons. He's not picking up pebbles to deposit in his craw to grind up the food he swallows. We *still* don't know if he tastes!"

Michael: "Maybe Pulu's got tastebuds in his gizzard!"

Having been the first to notice the juvenile feathers pushing out the fluffy down, Alison kept close watch and called their attention to the changes from day to day. For a time the baby fluff remained attached to the feathers and gave Pulu a rumpled, scruffy look.

"I suppose she's entering bird adolescence," she said somewhat ruefully. "She was such a cute baby!"

In the next few weeks Philip's boundless curiosity made him experiment to see if Pulu was indeed deeply ingrained with a fowl-principle that forbade him to eat the flesh of his own kind. Pulu was offered duck, goose, and turkey but refused them all. It made no difference whether the poultry was baked or broiled, braised or barbecued, stewed or deep-fat fried. It did not make any difference if it was soused with sauces, sprinkled with black, red, or white pepper or paprika, or flavored with garlic or sage. Pulu steadfastly refused to eat his own kind.

At the same time Philip satisfied his passion for knowing whens, whys, and wherefores. Taking breaks from writing his

25

book in a carrel in the university library, he looked up all the information about chukar partridges that he could find. It was not much, but whatever he found he brought home and shared with the family. One evening at the dinner table he picked Pulu up and lifted one of his feet.

"Notice Pulu's hind toe. The fourth toe is shorter than the three front ones. That's for running up steep slopes. Chukars escape their enemies downhill by flying but uphill by running. If they are alarmed they rise fast with strong rapid wing beats."

Michael: "I wonder when Pulu will fly!"

Melanie: "I hope never! She might fly away."

Philip: "He'll fly soon enough. You might be interested in knowing that the white meat on the breast of game birds is really only the two principal muscles that move the wings in a downward stroke."

Alison: "You've said just about enough to make me a vegetarian for life! I don't quite relish that worm of knowledge you brought home to feed your nestlings."

Philip: "Just one more worm. The reason Pulu is so smart and independent is that chukar partridges develop longer and in larger eggs in order to get a lively brain, strong legs, and a coat of feathers."

The feathers gradually thrust out the fluffy down, and Pulu began to look like a handsome juvenile. But whether he/she was male or female was still a riddle. Michael and Melanie were quarreling about it one day when Philip arrived home.

Michael : "Dad, Melanie and Mom keep on with this SHE—SHE—HER—HER talk! Anyone can see that Pulu is a HE."

Melanie: "Grandpa says that if Pulu were a HE, SHE would have grown a comb by this time. Look! Do you see anything that looks like a comb on Pulu's head? OK! Pulu is a SHE!"

Alison: "Melanie is right! A cock has a comb. No comb, no cock!"

26

Alison grabbed Melanie's hands and swung her into a ring dance around Pulu.

> Ha—Ha—Ha—HAHA!
> Ha—Ha—Ha—HAHA!
> Pulu's not a cock!
> Pulu is a HEN-N-N!

Philip: "Whoa, now, girls! Don't get so cockeyed cocky! Guess what I learned today? Even expert ornithologists find it hard to distinguish between male and female chukar partridges. The cock does not grow a comb. Nor does he grow the usual gorgeous fancy stuff that makes a male bird such a show-off. The male chukar has nothing to crow about. So we still don't know whether Pulu is a male or a female. We won't know until—"

Alison: "Until Pulu lays an egg! Will Melanie and I ever crow when that day comes, as come it will! As for Pulu not having anything to show off! Look at her! Look at her legs! They're changing from baby tan to dark brown, almost black. And they're going to end up being crimson-red. And the eyerims, too, are going to become crimson-red and stay crimson-red. And see the colors beginning to develop on her wings and tail and body! See those bars of buff, black, and chestnut beginning to appear! See that black band beginning to form across her forehead right through the eyes and down the sides of her neck. Before long Pulu will be wearing a beautiful necklace!"

Melanie: "And boys don't wear necklaces!"

Philip: "Don't be so sure, Melanie! You should see what some of the guys in my creative writing course come up with. They put more crazy creativity into their frippery than the Creator put on the peacock."

Pulu's wing feathers grew longer, stronger, and more colorful.

27

"A fashion designer couldn't do nearly as well," marveled Alison. "Pulu is absolutely original without being bizarre. Pulu, you are one stunning bird!"

Michael: "Do you suppose he knows it, Mom? Is that why he spends so much time combing his feathers? Maybe Pulu *is* a girl! They spend most of their time on their hair, don't they, Dad?"

Philip: "Not the women in our house. They don't have to do anything to make themselves beautiful. They already are!"

The next day Philip came home excitedly carrying a photocopy of a drawing of a larger-than-life bird feather.

"Please get the magnifying glass we gave you for your birthday, Kids, and we'll look at one of Pulu's new feathers."

Pulu chirped a shrill note of surprise when Philip pulled out one of his feathers.

"It's all right, Pulu. You'll soon grow a replacement."

Philip squinted through the magnifying glass at the feather and became almost poetic.

"What an intricacy is a bird's feather! As for preening, we've got it all wrong! We all supposed that Pulu is pluming his plumage, grooming himself to look well groomed. Everyone else must think the same, for the word 'preening' has come to mean primping. 'Tain't that at all! Come here and look! Do you see those winglike vanes going off from the central shaft?"

The twins were not sure that they did but as usual pretended that they did.

"See those delicate branches or barbs that make the vane? Look closer. Your naked eye can't see the tiny hooks that lock the barbs together and make the feather elastic and strong. They interlock like zippers. But they can come unhooked and have to be hooked up again."

"So that's what Pulu is doing when we accuse her of trying to make herself pretty!" laughed Alison. "She's hooking up the zillions of hooks on her feathers!"

28

Michael: "I wish I were a bird and didn't have to go to school to learn how to solve problems! Pulu is born with everything in his head."

Alison: "Lucky, lucky Pulu! She doesn't have to beat out her brains to fix zippers!"

On one perfect Sunday afternoon the four Malechas and Pulu went hiking all around in Noe Woods at the arboretum. As a rule Pulu followed closely behind them on his walks with them, but sometimes he chased after a butterfly or moth and disappeared. If they got too far ahead of him, he scolded. But today he had disappeared more than usual under hazelnut and blackberry bushes. When he reappeared and they tried to carry him, he fluttered out of their hands to the path. He should by rights have been too tired to do what he did later that night after a Sunday supper of celery, cheese, and nuts eaten informally at the kitchen counter. But he showed no signs of being tired.

"I don't know about the rest of you," said Philip, "but I feel like watching a movie on VCR tonight. How about *Shane*? And I'm going to do it lying down!"

Inside the TV room, Philip sprawled on the couch. Because he was six feet two he dangled his right leg on the floor and pulled his left leg up. Pulu promptly ran up his right leg and perched on his left knee, riveting his eyes on Alison, who sat across the room in an armchair. Suddenly he stepped into the air and just as suddenly discovered the buoyancy of air and the fact of his wings. His wings fluttered wildly but fearlessly. They held their breaths until Pulu was safely perched on Alison's shoulder.

"He did it! He did it!" cried Michael.

"Oh, marvelous!" whispered Alison. "Pulu's first flight!"

Summer Adventures

Although Pulu soon mastered the art of flying, he remained true to his chukar partridge nature and proved to be more of a runner than a flier. The twins' fears that he might fly away were soon dispelled. Pulu's bond to each of them was so strong that they could entrust him with complete freedom indoors and outdoors without worrying that he would stray perversely, intentionally, rashly, capriciously, or purely unintentionally. His urge to follow them was so strong that they could take him for walks in the arboretum quite confident that he would not get lost. At the age of four weeks Pulu was approximately four inches tall and could not see or be seen above the grasses, weeds, and prairie flowers. Yet, although he stopped often to peck at ants, bugs, dirt, seeds, pebbles, and the like, he tagged after the twins unerringly. They could follow his progress by the movement of the plants as he bumped against the stems. At times he would hop up on a stump or fallen branch to reconnoiter, correct his bearings with relation to the twins, and then dive into the vegetation again. If they tried to carry him, he tolerated it for a while but soon squirmed out of their hands, choosing to follow them rather than to be carried by them.

It did not take long for them to learn Pulu's favorite areas in the arboretum. He preferred the drylands to the wetlands, the dry lime prairie to the wet prairie, the sandy knolls north of Green Prairie to the cattail marsh and sedge meadow in Gardner Marsh.

"I'm sure it's Pulu's ancestral memory that makes her prefer drylands to wetlands," said Alison. "The Arb is a far cry from the steep, rocky Himalayan slopes, but Pulu's instincts are with the more open and barren parts of it."

"The chukar is known as the barren country bird. It's sometimes called the bird that lives on nothing," said Philip, who was reading all the books on Asian birds that he could find in all the libraries in Madison and was even having computers searching every library in the country.

Pulu's first grasshopper leaped with a snapping of wings in front of them one July day when they took a walk along the firelanes that crisscrossed Curtis Prairie. Pulu caught it on the wing but did not swallow it until he had plucked off its legs and wings.

Michael: "I'll bet he does that because they would tickle his stomach."

Melanie: "I wonder what grasshoppers taste like! Potato chips?"

Michael: "Chocolate-covered peanuts?"

Pulu quickly revealed a preference for dry and crunchy rather than damp and moist foods. Nuts were the most pleasing

32

to his palate. Celery and cheese were the moistest foods he tolerated, and sticky and gummy foods displeased him as much as they displease people with partial plates. After being persuaded to try oatmeal, he spent ten minutes wiping his bill on Michael's sweatshirt. Ice cream was the only wet food he relished, and with what relish!

"Tom couldn't believe his eyes today when we came in after our bike ride and fixed ourselves doubledips. Pulu sat on my shoulder and shared mine with me."

Pulu's main diet continued to be pelletized duck food, but he continued to supplement that rather dull diet with more stomach-stirring food. Fly swatters and insecticides (which were never permitted in that household anyway) were unnecessary, for Pulu searched out every ant, spider, wood tick, mosquito, or fly that found its way into the house. When Philip, a born-and-brought-up wood scavenger, placed a chunk of gangrenous oak in the fireplace and it suddenly exploded ants, Pulu disposed of them in no time.

"May she have no fluttering in her stomach!" Alison wished fervently.

Since Pulu's diet provided sufficient green vegetation for him to be "in the green," his pecking at the plants in the mini-arboretum was perhaps motivated more by his instinct than by a nutritional deficiency. When Alison saw him pecking Moses out of her Moses-in-the-bulrushes plant, though, she sternly told him to stop.

"Pulu, NO! Stop it!"

Pulu did stop, but only for a time. He began again and now chucked a new sound that Alison labeled, "I know I'm being naughty, but—!"

Pulu also pecked at newsprint, showing a slight preference for the Democratic *Capital Times* over the Republican *Wisconsin State Journal*.

33

"I wonder how Pulu can digest what's printed in most newspapers," said Philip.

They permitted his consumption of newspapers, but when he began to find book jackets tasty and would not heed their "NO! Stop it, Pulu!" Philip turned him upside down and lightly spanked him. The twins were horrified.

"You never spank *us*, Dad!"

"No, and I never will. Spanking debases the human spanker as well as the human being spanked. Not so with birds. I'm not hurting Pulu. I'm just trying to tell him that some behavior is not acceptable."

Pulu, rightside up again, jumped on the coffee table and joyously resumed pecking the dust jacket of Gabriel Garcia Marquez's *Collected Stories*, a jacket splashed with colorful, exotic Colombian plants.

"Pulu thinks it's a game, Dad!" chortled Michael.

"I'm afraid Michael is right," said Alison. "This is a wonderful new game that gives Pulu the attention she craves."

"Maybe," said Melanie, "if we don't pay any attention to her pecking plants and books she'll quit."

For one week the Melanie policy was put into action. Or one could say inaction, for they all held their tongues and turned their backs or walked away when Pulu pecked at plants and print. By the end of the week Pulu had more or less lost interest in denuding plants and consuming book jackets.

Philip and Perry began taking Pulu on their frequent early-evening circle runs around the Fish Hatchery and back along the shore of Lake Wingra. One evening Philip returned carrying Pulu in his cupped hands.

"Pulu just had a huge fright near Red Wing Marsh. A hawk took off from a branch of a dead tree and flew in a circle over our heads. It was flying rather low. Pulu let out a cry he has never

34

made before. Perry and I stopped, and Pulu scurried and fluttered into my hands. He was one frightened bird!"

"Could a hawk pick up Pulu and carry him away? And eat him?" Michael asked anxiously.

"It sure could, and so could golden eagles and great horned owls and falcons. Not to speak of fox, coyotes, wolves, cats, and dogs! Even in this nature paradise Pulu has his enemies."

Michael: "Yes, but Pulu has never seen a hawk! How does he know that they are dangerous?"

Philip: "Ancestral memory again, Michael! Perry said that Pulu's ancient chukar memory was telling him that it was either a Himalayan Golden Eagle or a Shahen Falcon. Both of them feed on chukar partridges. Swoop down from a great height and strike with powerful claws."

Alison: "Poor Pulu! To be haunted by such fears!"

They all heard Pulu's low-pitched, undulating fear cry the next morning shortly after he begged to go out on his own brief forage for food. The twins ran out and scanned the sky.

"No hawks, owls, eagles, or herons in sight," Melanie called to the parents.

"No vultures or ospreys, either," called Michael, who was rapidly developing his father's quixotic sense of humor.

Not to be outdone, Melanie cried, "Not any dragonflies either. It's a false alarm."

"Don't be too sure of that," said Philip, coming out of the house. "Pulu saw something alarming up there and is still seeing it. Alison, please fetch the telescope."

Philip pointed the telescope skyward and let out a whoop.

"It's a weather balloon! Pulu's deadly enemy is a weather-monitoring balloon!"

"Golly, what peepers that bird's got!" marveled Michael.

Pulu's strangest fear response happened on a leisurely

Sunday afternoon drive around Lake Mendota and Lake Monona. The ultimate goal was ice cream cones, and because Pulu was crazy about ice cream cones they took him along. It was his first car ride, but he quickly tuned in to the new experience, hopped on Philip's left shoulder, and braced himself against Philip's shoulder on the curves.

"I think our youngest is going to be a great traveler, Alison!"

Suddenly Pulu gave a short guttural "kerr" sound and hopped to the floor, frantically seeking a hiding place.

"Now whatever caused that? Do you spot anything, Kids?"

"Not even a weather balloon, Dad."

After a few miles Pulu came out from behind the children's feet, hopped up on Philip's left shoulder, and resumed his interested surveillance of the scenery that was so strangely whizzing by him. Suddenly he was on the floor again, kerring with fear.

"Dad, I think I know what scared him," cried Michael. "Both times we went under an overpass."

"Sure enough! He's afraid of the shadow of the bridge!"

Eventually they learned to trust Pulu's fear calls, even if most of the time he was mistakenly alarmed and the fearful unknown turned out to be a low-flying airplane, the sudden disappearance of the sun behind a cloud, or anything else that suddenly presented a silhouette that in his collective memory might be a Himalayan Golden Eagle, a Shahen Falcon, or even a Griffin Vulture. Pulu for his part learned to trust their, "It's only a bridge," and to be reassured by the quiet announcement, "Bridge coming up, Pulu!"

They also learned to know and trust Pulu's night vision. Late one moonless night Pulu gave his fear call in their living room. They turned on the outdoor lights, and there on a post sat a barred owl in the process of eating a mouse it had just caught. Another time it was a screech owl sitting in the dark on the railing of the deck.

"Here's a riddle for you kids," said Philip. "If I say that Pulu is owl-eyed, do I mean that he's dim-visioned as an owl in daylight or sharp-visioned as an owl in the dark?"

"Dim," said Melanie.

"Sharp," said Michael.

"Look it up!" said Philip, who did not believe in giving all the answers all the time.

Melanie and Michael began begging to take Pulu along to the public beach on the far side of Lake Wingra.

"Please, Mom and Dad! The kids are crazy about him! We'll all watch him like a hawk. Oops! Sorry, Pulu! We'll leave out the hawk!"

"But Pulu dislikes wetness! What is she going to do while you all are swimming?"

"Don't worry, Mom. Pulu always finds something to do."

So, for the first time out of his egg Pulu found sand. Dry sand in the sun. Dry, light, fine, sun-warmed sand! Pulu promptly knew exactly what to do. He chuckled and chortled and chukared his happiest sounds. He dove into the dry, sun-warmed sand and began "dusting" as his ancestors had been doing for centuries on the south side of high Himalayan ridges. He went at it as easily and vigorously as if it were a daily occurrence in his life, a well-developed habit.

First of all Pulu pecked up a small mound of sand under his breast, then with his right foot flipped it under his left wing and up over the top of his back. Then he pecked up another little mound of sand and with his left foot flipped it up under his right wing and over his back. When he wearied of it, he spread out his wings and sprawled in a kind of panting ecstasy—only to begin dusting all over again. When the twins had had enough of swimming, Pulu had not had enough of dusting. He had to be carried home, complaining all the way. The sound was as close to a growl as a bird can sound.

The next day the twins and their friends discovered the game of "Burying Pulu." They scooped out a hole in the sand and covered him with sand up to his creamy white chin. Pulu lay perfectly still. Then, suddenly, with a happy chukar chuckle he exploded from his sand capsule and ran around in circles beating his wings. It was difficult to tell who was having more fun—Pulu or the children. He came back to their hands again and again for a repeat performance. The children eventually wearied of the game, but not Pulu. He was still grumbling when they arrived home. Alison cuddled him close.

"Oh, Pulu, you old grouser, you!"

Philip disappeared into his study and came back with a puzzled look on his face.

"The word 'grousing' seems to have nothing to do with grouse. It's from 'grutch,' an Old English word meaning to grumble and complain. The word 'grouch' also comes from it."

"But Pulu is neither a grouse nor a grouch," said Alison, stroking Pulu's grumbling into contented sounds.

In late summer, when beaches were no longer inviting to humans, Pulu discovered that the ashes in the fireplace were entirely suitable for dusting. Lukewarm or cold ashes, that is. He dramatically learned to be wary of fireplaces after backing too close to the flames on one of the first cool and rainy evenings in August. So close that his tail feathers caught fire. Fortunately, feathers, like pure and unadulterated wool, are not highly combustible, and his cries of alarm brought swift rescue.

"I hope that teaches you a lesson, Pulu. From now on stay away from fire," said Alison.

"Lady Bird, Lady Bird,/ Fly away home./ Your house is on fire/ And your children will burn," chanted Melanie.

38

"It's Lady BUG, Lady BUG!" said Michael. "Besides, Pulu is not a lady."

"Here we go again!" groaned Philip.

Morning-after ashes, Pulu soon learned, were safe for dusting and did precisely what sand seemed to do for him—make his unclean and unkempt self feel clean and kempt again. The sand or ash baths were always followed by an hour or so of preening—which, please remember, is not a prideful primping but is the arranging of the disarranged barbules on the barbs of his feathers.

Camping with Pulu

Should they or should they not take Pulu along on their annual camping trip the last two weeks in August? Long before Pulu had entered their lives, they had planned a circle tour of Lake Superior.

"That means taking Pulu across the U.S.-Canadian border twice!" worried Alison. "I've heard that customs officials get pretty sticky about pets. What if they won't let us take Pulu across into Canada?"

"What if they let us take her across and then won't let us take her back?" worried Melanie.

"That reminds me of a true story I read somewhere but can't remember where," said Philip. "It was about a Texas family that spent some time up in the Canadian Arctic tundra. They adopted a dozen snow goose goslings that for some reason had been hatched too late to join the flock migrating south. When the time came for the family to leave they decided to bring the orphans back to Texas with them in their panel truck. By the time they reached the border the goslings had learned to fly and had also developed a strong bond to their human family. The bond was mutual, and the family was dismayed to be told by the customs officials that they would have to leave the geese in Canada because they had no exit visa for them. There was nothing to do but release the birds, say a tearful goodbye to them, drive across the border and on to Texas."

"Oh, the meanies! The horrid meanies!" sputtered Melanie.

"What else could they do, Melanie?"

"I mean the customs officials."

"Customs officials have strict rules and regulations made for our protection, and they have to follow them. But the story isn't over. The panel truck crossed the border and drove on down the highway. But the twelve goslings had no intention of being left behind. They took to the air, followed the truck, and flew across the border. You see, there is no law forbidding birds to do that. The Texans stopped the truck a mile or so down the highway and took their snow goslings in again."

Determined to forestall any and every possible obstruction, Philip investigated all the formalities of the laws regarding the transportation of pets across national borders and observed them all. They arrived at Sault Ste. Marie with all the proper papers.

As it turned out, the feathered "goods" they declared ruffled no official feathers and merely collected an interested and fascinated audience. Even an official so gruff and tough he would scare veteran smugglers of contraband melted before Pulu, excitedly called on his intercom, and told everyone to come see the pet an American family was taking across.

"By George," he exclaimed incredulously, "this has got to be a first! As far as I know, no partridge has ever come across this border."

"Not even—?" began Michael, intending to tease the officer about birds that *flew* across the border, but a sharp nudge from Philip silenced him.

"Never, never try to tease cops, corporals, or any other of their bureaucratic kin," Philip advised him later on the Canadian side.

Pulu created mini-sensations with campers as well as border officials and rapidly became the pet of the campgrounds at which they stayed. Except early in the morning, when he wandered around the campgrounds chucking the chukar partridge early morning rally call to all other partridges, near and far. The call begins with a long, slow "chuck, chuck, chuck"—a break between each chuck. It rises in intensity and becomes a two-syllable "per-chuck, per-chuck." At its highest intensity it has three syllables: "chuck-a-ra, chuck-a-ra." The twins interpreted that to mean, "Here I am! Where are you?"

When other campers complained about being awakened so early, it was decided that Pulu not be allowed out of the sleeping bag he happened to be sharing before the smoke of the first campfire was seen in the morning. Having made that decision they all looked at Alison, who after the first week of camping was the only one who would allow Pulu into her sleeping bag.

Philip: "He's got this instinct to set his nest in order, and he thinks the hairs on my chest are grass and turns and turns and pecks at them for about five minutes before he settles down."

Michael: "Every time I turn over he growls."

Melanie: "She growls when she gets tangled in my hair."

Alison: "So dear, sweet, uncomplaining Mom gets to have Pulu as bedmate! Why can't she roost on a tree branch?"

Philip: "Chukar partridges don't roost."

Alison: "Why don't we get her her own sleeping bag?"

Michael: "Mom, he's scared of the dark, especially when he's in a strange place."

Melanie: "I am, too, sort of. I like to be close to you and Dad."

Alison: "OK, Pulu. It looks as if we two are sleeping partners for the rest of the trip!"

Back in the United States again, on the Minnesota side of Lake Superior, it was Pulu's presence that saved them from a stiff traffic fine. Because the Gooseberry Falls campground was so popular, they had made a reservation three months in advance for the weekend of August 23. But along the way down the north shore of Lake Superior they had stopped too many times to explore the mouths of the whitewater rivers, and now it was beginning to get dark.

"We might lose our campsite!" said Philip, pressing his foot on the gas pedal and accelerating to seventy miles an hour. "Watch out for a highway patrol car, Kids."

But a patrol car lurking behind the garbage cans at a rest stop pulled onto the highway behind them, chased them with flashing lights, and signaled them to pull over and stop. The officer was polite but firm.

"I'm sorry, but you were going fifteen miles over the speed limit."

Pulu, who was sleeping in his favorite place, on the driver's left shoulder, began to chuck his irritation at being awakened.

"Whazzat?" asked the patrolman, his pencil poised in midair.

Philip quietly introduced him to Pulu, who promptly demonstrated his friendship by pecking at the officer's badge and plucking his pencil from his fingers.

"Well, whaddyaknow!" exclaimed the patrolman. "But,"

44

he continued, almost reluctantly, "I will have to give you a warning ticket."

They had cooked all their meals at campgrounds or had lunched in the car on fruit and cheese and crackers, but on the home stretch they stopped at a restaurant on Lake Pepin that friends had told them never to pass by if they were within a hundred miles of it.

"Are we going to leave Pulu in the car?" asked Melanie as Alison was parking as near to the Harbor View Cafe as she could get.

Philip: "Some restaurants have signs saying, 'No shirt, no shoes, no food,' but I've never seen a sign saying 'No partridges.' "

Michael: "I'll take Pulu for a walk along the Mississippi River and the rest of you can eat in the restaurant. Pulu and I don't like snooty restaurants."

Melanie: "I don't either. Besides, they probably won't let Pulu in, and I don't want her to be embarrassed."

Alison: "Does this look like a snooty restaurant? To me it looks as if it could be called Grandma's Cafe with a sign saying, 'We Specialize In Homecooked Food.' "

Michael: "I'll bet it's such a snobby place the waiter would sneer if I ordered pizza."

Alison: "Come along and try it! Pulu loves pizza, and I'm sure she'll wipe the sneer off anyone's face."

After flutter-flying down the block to the restaurant and exercising his wings, Pulu followed them so quietly into the crowded restaurant that no one noticed him.

"A table for five, please," said Philip to the plump and pleasant headwaitress who came forward and ushered them to the only table in the room that was unoccupied. It was set for four.

45

"Five?"

Alison stooped to pick up Pulu.

"Yes, please. We are five."

"Oh, of course! Andy, will you please set another place at this table?"

Neither the headwaitress nor the waiter raised an eyebrow as Pulu hopped to the chair and onto the table. There were murmurs of surprise and some startled laughter at the other tables, but no one threatened to walk out if that hen or whatever it was was permitted to stay.

Waiter: "Would you like something to drink before your lunch?"

Philip: "Just water, please."

Michael: "No ice for Pulu, please. He doesn't like ice water."

Waiter: "He's a very wise bird. Our soup today is Dibs and Dabs of Everything Soup."

Alison: "That sounds wonderful. Shall we all have soup?"

Michael: "Pulu won't eat it if it has dibs and dabs of any kind of poultry in it."

Waiter: "I cannot tell a lie. I suspect it has chicken backs and necks in it. The chef could send someone quickly to catch some grasshoppers along the railroad tracks and could deep fry them for Pulu."

Philip: "Thank you! Very gracious of you to offer that, I must say! I'd be tempted to try deep-fried grasshoppers myself. But Pulu will be happy with pieces of celery and cheese and some nuts. Could he have pizza for the main course?"

Michael: "Pizza for me, too."

Melanie: "For me, too, please."

The twins watched for a curling of the waiter's lip, but the curving stretched ever upward and threatened to crack the waiter's cheeks.

Alison: "It won't be any trouble for the chef to make a special order of pizza, will it? The children are rather conventional eaters and will enjoy pizza more than the menu for today written on the blackboard. My husband and I, of course, are eager to try your blanquette de veau."

Waiter: "No trouble at all, Ma'am! Our chef loves to get pizza orders so that he can throw all the powers of his imagination into a pizza that makes anything else by that name a bad joke."

Michael, with some alarm, asked him to tell the chef not to make the pizza too, TOO creative.

While the others ate their soup, Pulu thirstily drank water from his glass and neatly picked up nuts, sesame seeds, and pieces of celery. Several departing diners stopped at the table to ask questions about him. Needless to say, Philip reveled in the opportunity to lecture on the wild bird that Marco Polo had encountered on the roof of the world. When the waiter finally brought the order, he had to disperse the fascinated audience with a waiterly cough and an unwaiterly jest.

"Ladies and Gentlemen, I could do a scriptural stunt and lower this food to the table from the ceiling, but it might just tip and dump, and I would not enjoy being responsible."

The twins proclaimed the pizza crust the crispiest and the sauce the zestiest and the pizza topping the best they had ever eaten. As for the veal stew with the fancy name of "blanquette de veau," Alison could only close her eyes and murmur, "This sauce! This sauce! Jane Brody and Irma Rombauer, you have been bested! Nothing I have made out of your cookbooks ever tasted like this!"

Pulu sat between the twins in the back seat between Pepin and Madison, and the three of them slept all the way home. That is, Pulu slept until the car turned onto McCaffrey Drive, when he leaped to Philip's shoulder and chuck-kerred with excitement. He flew out the open window as the car passed Red Wing Marsh and disappeared into the cattails and thickets of red osier dogwood.

"Pulu, come back!" called Alison.

"Don't worry, dear! He'll come home. He's just glad to be back in his Arb!"

Pulu was now a beautiful, full-grown chukar partridge, streamlined, and weighing about nineteen ounces. His cheeks and throat were creamy white, his diagonal striping bold and black, and his beak and legs orange-red. Without a running start and without opening his wings he could jump three-and-a-half feet in the air. When he opened his wings and flew he could attain an amazing velocity.

"The speed of a chukar partridge in flight has not been clocked," Philip told them after coming home one day from his carrel in the university library, "but it is said to equal the highest speed in game birds."

True to his chukar nature, Pulu preferred to walk or to run. Early one evening Philip and the twins took him to Fish Hatchery Road to clock his running speed.

"Fifteen miles an hour, Mom!" Melanie announced on their return.

"Eighteen! I was closer to the speedometer than you, and the needle touched eighteen twice!"

By Labor Day Pulu's affection for his human family was as full-grown and beautiful as his body. Moreover, it was equally divided among them. Asleep or awake, he wanted to be with one of them or all of them, preferably with all four of them together. His craving for togetherness had been quite satisfied throughout the summer, especially on the camping trip, and he was totally unprepared for the absence of all four of them now that schools were starting. His tiny but intelligent bird brain did

48

not grasp that the spacious wire pen being built on the ground floor was for him in bad weather and that the south wing of the deck was being screened for him to use in good weather. Not until the rainy September day they shut him in the indoor pen with his food, water, and playthings and went their various ways.

"Pulu, Pulu," crooned Alison, giving him a last cuddle, "we hate to do this to you, but we just can't leave you at large all day while we are gone. This is the safest place for you until we come home."

"Goodbye, Pulu! Be a good bird while we are gone!" Michael and Melanie called back from the door.

After two such leavetakings and daylong confinements, Pulu began playing a game that would have been jolly fun had it not entailed being late for classes and work. After eating his breakfast of scrambled eggs and Oscar Mayer sausage with them on the third morning, he vanished. In his shrewd little bird brain he reasoned that if he could not be found, his family could not leave. So he disappeared. For the next few mornings he disappeared under beds and couches, in kitchen cabinets and closets, inside laundry tubs and clothes baskets, behind the backpacks and hiking boots, behind skis and toboggans. He crouched and froze in his hiding place while they frantically or exasperatedly or sometimes angrily searched for him.

"Pulu, come here at once, or I'll wring your neck!" shouted Philip, quite illogically, for of course he could not wring Pulu's neck if Pulu did not come.

They soon learned to know all of Pulu's hiding places, however, and were able to capture and confine him in time to make their classes. Although he never ceased playing the hide-and-seek game, Pulu learned to accept the inevitable internment and to wait for the joy of weekend togetherness. On the

49

rare occasions when one of them was ill and had to stay home, Pulu was beside himself with joy and never left the sick one's side.

"Was Pulu a nuisance?" Alison asked when she returned at the end of a day Philip had stayed home with strep throat.

"That's what's so amazing! He seemed to sense that he should be a quiet presence and not a chatty companion. I must say he was very comforting."

Not long afterward Alison herself experienced Pulu's solicitous companionship beside (or *on*) the sick bed.

"I can't think of any human being I could tolerate sticking so close when I feel wretchedly sick," she told Philip and the twins when they came home. "Not even you precious ones."

"That's OK, Mom. Why don't you have Pulu bring you your toast and tea?" teased Michael.

"And rub your back and straighten your sheets?" added Philip.

Pulu's affection for his human family was neither addictive nor exclusive. He enjoyed the twins' friends and their comings and goings as much as the twins did. At the dinner and cocktail parties Alison and Philip gave that autumn, Pulu quickly found the friendliest shoulder and rode around in style, accepting cracked walnuts from any and all hands. He was especially attracted to delicately scented female guests, and after snuggling a whole evening against a perfumed earlobe would himself smell distinctly pleasant for a few days.

"Why do I think of Nicole Dubois every time Pulu lands on my shoulder?" asked Philip the day after they had entertained his department at a cocktail party during Thanksgiving break.

"Because they both smell of Gauloise, *un parfum affranchi*," said Alison.

50

A Christmas Visitor

On December 24 Babička [Ba-beơrh'-ka], the lively Czechoslovakian Catholic grandmother, Philip's mother, came from California for her annual Christmas visit. All the Malechas went to meet her at the Madison airport. All, that is, but Pulu. Although he behaved so beautifully in public nowadays that they took him almost everywhere, they were fearful of the airport crowds hurrying to get somewhere for Christmas.

"Some human giant might accidentally step on his toes. For a bird to injure or lose one toe is a serious handicap," said Philip.

Instead of running to meet them at the door when the five of them returned, Pulu flew to the highest branch of the Christmas tree they had cut at a tree farm that morning and had set up but not yet trimmed. He perched there silently and solemnly, as

53

if posing for a picture. Babička laughed so hard that tears rolled down her cheeks.

"So this is Pulu!" she said when she was able to talk. "From all you have written to me, I know he's the most intelligent bird in the world, but please don't try to tell me that you have taught him 'The Twelve Days of Christmas'! Surely he isn't posing as a partridge in a Christmas tree for want of a pear tree!"

"No, we didn't teach Pulu 'The Twelve Days of Christmas' because we don't believe the partridge-in-the-pear-tree bit," said Philip. "Partridges don't roost. Come here, Pulu, and meet Babička."

Philip held out his left arm and Pulu flew down from the Christmas tree, perched on his wrist, and scanned Babička with bright beady eyes.

"A hen or a cock?"

"A cock," said Michael.

"A hen!" said Melanie.

"I see," said Babička. "It seems that we have a mystery. Wonderful! I love mysteries! Pulu, you riddle bird, I brought you a gift. I made it myself especially for you."

Babička fumbled in her purse and pulled out a necklace made of seeds and nuts. She hung it on Pulu's neck.

"It's a rosary, Pulu. The seeds are the Aves and the nuts are the Paternosters and the Glorias."

"But Pulu will eat her rosary!" gasped Melanie.

"That's quite all right, Melanie, dear. Prayers should not only come from the inner being, they should go to the inner being."

Pulu of course did eat his rosary immediately and from that hour and forever after considered Babička just one rung below the rest of the family on his ladder of love. In fact, to everyone's surprise, he slept at the foot of her bed throughout the twelve days of her visit.

54

Pulu was the only one who was allowed to stay in the guest room and watch Babička unpack her two bulging bags and mysterious boxes.

"The stewardess glared at all my carry-on baggage," she told the family when they helped bring all her bags and boxes to her room. "But I had slipped my false teeth into my purse when they called my plane, and my mouth was sunken in. I stooped and walked with a limp. I boarded the plane with the mothers with babies and the passengers in wheelchairs. After a second look at me, the stewardess quit glaring and helped me store everything up above. She helped me off, too. A really lovely girl she was, God bless her!"

"I have yet to decide, Mother of mine, whether you are full of Bohemian gypsy trickiness or of just plain mischief," said Philip.

After they had trimmed the Christmas tree, they all attended a candlelight service in the Lutheran church with Bestemor and Grandpa Mason and then came back to have Christmas Eve supper with Pulu. What a feast it proved to be when all the foods Bestemor and Babička brought were put together with what the others had prepared!

"I don't know which I like better," said Michael, "Bestemor's kringla or Babička's kolache."

"I don't know what I like better, Bestemor's lefse or Babička's Christmas bread," said Melanie.

"It's not a Czech bread. It's a German bread called Christstollen because if it's braided right it looks like the Christ Child in swaddling clothes."

"Babička, you always see deep-down meanings in everything," said Alison. "Bestemor, does lefse have any symbolism to Norwegians?"

Bestemor's blue eyes twinkled.

"It reminds them that once they were so poor that they

only had potatoes and a little flour to eat. So they put them together and got lefse."

If Pulu showed any partiality, it was for Bestemor's Swedish meatballs.

"She's a wise bird, Mother," said Alison. "These are the best you have ever made."

"I ought to be able to make good meatballs after making them every Christmas Eve day for fifty years!"

"What was the traditional Christmas Eve meat in Czechoslovakia?" Grandpa Mason asked Babička.

"Fish, not meat. On Christmas Eve we ate carp."

"Carp!" exclaimed Grandpa Mason. "That common, low-down—!" He stopped suddenly. "Sorry, Ma'am! I don't mean to be disrespectful, but in this country—"

"I know! I know!" said Babička crisply. "You don't respect carp in this country, but in Czechoslovakia we respect carp so much that we eat it on the night of Christ's birth."

"Well," said Philip, "carp can't be any humbler than lutefisk, which is the Norwegian's lowliest fish preserved in a lye solution. You all know, of course, that we open stopped-up drains with lye."

"I've never liked lutefisk," said Alison, "and that's why we don't have it tonight."

"The only thing wrong with this wonderful meal," muttered Grandpa, who was not even Norwegian.

Before they opened their gifts, they read the Christmas story and sang Christmas carols in three languages. Alison, Philip, and the twins sang "Silent Night." Bestemor and Grandpa and Alison sang "Stille Nat." Babička and Philip sang "Ticha' noc."

Song after song they sang that way and were so carried away that they forgot the presents under the tree. When they were singing "Joy to the World" Pulu once again flew to the top of the Christmas tree and began to chuck.

56

"Don't stop singing," said Philip in a low voice, "but pay attention to Pulu. I think he's chucking in time to the music!"

It did indeed seem that when they sang, "Repeat the sounding joy, Repeat the sounding joy," Pulu sang, "Chuck, chuck, chuck, chuck, chuck, chuck! Chuck, chuck, chuck, chuck, chuck, chuck!"

"The first day of Christmas—a partridge in a pear tree—" mused Babička. "We'll really have to look into that! I feel there's something secret hiding in that song!"

At ten o'clock Bestemor and Grandpa went home, Pulu went to sleep, and the rest of them went to midnight mass. Melanie felt such a strange and wonderful joy standing beside Babička hearing the good news of Christ being born, singing all the Alleluias, and smelling the fragrance of incense. At times like this, she wished they always went to the Catholic church and not just when Babička was there. Just a week before she had told Michael that she would rather be a Catholic than a Lutheran, and he had laughed at her.

"That's because you like poems and flowers and cry over movies on TV."

"It is not!" she had flashed back angrily.

"OK, why?"

"If I could tell you you wouldn't understand anyway!"

Babička went to mass again on Christmas morning, but the twins slept until Pulu lightly but impatiently pecked them awake. They were sleepy and irritable until they looked outside and saw that three inches of snow had fallen during the night.

"Wow! Now we can use our new skis!"

Grandpa's farm with its gentle hills was a perfect place for beginners at skiing, and Bestemor's fruit soup and flatbread was a perfect meal after several hours out in the crisp air. Pulu became almost as excited about the dry fluffy snow as he had been when he discovered sand.

On St. Stephen's Day, Babička brought out small round

loaves of homeground whole wheat bread she had brought along and more kolache and koblihi and told them all over again about good King Wenceslaus, the Czech king who went to a poor man's hut on the Feast of Stephen. She sang the whole song to them in Czech and then had them sing it in dialogue, with Philip and Michael singing the King's part and Alison and Melanie and Babička singing the page's part. Once again Pulu flew to the top of the Christmas tree and chucked in time.

"Chuck, chuck, chuck, chuck, chuck, chuck, chuck!"

"Philip," said Babička, "please try to find some books in your library about birds in legends, myths, and folk stories. There simply has to be something about the partridge in the pear tree!"

The next day Philip spent a few hours on his book at the library and came home with two books: John Pollard's *Birds in Greek Life and Myth* and Beryl Rowland's *Birds with Human Souls*.

"See what you can find in these books."

"What intriguing titles!" exclaimed Babička, and promptly disappeared into her room and closed the door. Several hours later when they knocked at the door to invite her to dinner, she asked to be excused.

"I feel like a detective about to break a baffling murder case clean open. I think I'll have solved it in an hour or so."

Two hours later she joined them before the fire with the dazed look of someone who has been reading too hard and too long. Pulu promptly jumped on her lap. She stroked his head and looked at each one of them in turn as if she had not seen them for a very long time.

Babička: "Dearly beloveds, do you know what I am holding?"

Michael: "That's easy! Pulu, of course!"

Philip: "A chukar partridge."

58

Babička: "I am holding the most unjustly and malevolently maligned bird in the Kingdom of Birddom!"

Melanie: "What do those big words that start with *m* mean?"

Philip: "Babička means that long ago some people did a smear job on partridges and gave them a bad name."

Michael: "Who says?"

Babička: "The authors of both these books. I must say they seem to be excellent scholars."

Melanie: "As good as Daddy?"

Philip: "I have yet to make my dent in the world of scholarship, children."

Alison: "You will, dear! You will!"

Babička (almost fiercely): "Be quiet, all of you! Do you want to hear about how the ancient people felt about this beautiful bird?"

"We do! We do!" they chorused meekly.

"It seems they knew the chukar partridge in the Near East as well as in the Far East. There they regarded the partridge as tricky, treacherous, and thievish."

"Tricky and thievish!" exploded Michael. "Pulu has never stolen a thing in his life!"

Babička: "Tricky, treacherous, and thievish is bad enough, but to the ancients, partridges were the symbol of something even worse. They symbolized impure, lustful, wicked love. If Titian painted a partridge into his paintings, he put it there to personify lust."

Melanie: "What is lust?"

Michael: "Golly, don't you even know that?"

Philip: "OK, Michael, what is it?"

Michael: "Aw, *you* tell her!"

Philip: "All living bodies have a very strong hunger to join

59

in the making of new bodies. The act of joining is called sexual intercourse. Your mother and I had sexual intercourse and made you. When the hunger for sexual intercourse is selfish and self-gratifying and brutish and without love it can be called lust."

Melanie: "And partridges were supposed to be full of lust?"

Babička: "The ancients thought partridges were full of wicked lust. Even as late as the early twentieth century the word partridge in English slang meant 'whore.' "

Melanie: "What's a whore?"

Philip: "A woman who sells her body to satisfy men's lust."

Babička: "And not only was the partridge a symbol for wicked lust, partridges—or partridge cocks—were thought to be so sexually potent that if they just flew over a female partridge or crowed close enough for her to hear she became impregnated and would lay fertile eggs!"

Philip: "Hey, now! That rings a bell! Aristotle! I remember now that Aristotle mentioned something like that! I've got his complete works in my study. I think I can find it!"

In five minutes he was back in his chair with a volume of Aristotle.

"You are absolutely right, Mother! It's all here in Aristotle's *History of Animals*. Listen to these descriptions of the partridge: The female 'is affected by the voice of the male, or by his breathing down on her as he flies overhead.' 'As has been observed, the bird has mischievous and deceitful habits.' 'Owing to the lecherous nature of the bird. . . .' 'The general wicked habits of the bird. . . .' Pulu, Pulu, with the great Aristotle badmouthing your ancestors, no wonder partridges had a bad image!"

Alison: "But I don't see the connection to the pear tree!"

Babička: "Ah, but there *is* a connection! The pear tree, too,

60

is heavy with sexual symbolism. In fact, it was a very well known phallic symbol."

Melanie: "What's phallic?"

Philip: "*Phallos* is the Greek word for penis."

Babička: "The pear tree was so well known as a sexual symbol that pious people tried to change it in the song to a fig tree or a juniper tree or barley. But the public refused to sing 'A partridge in a juniper tree'—or 'in a fig tree.' "

Alison: "So! The lover's gift to the singer was not so intangible after all! I wonder if I can ever sing 'The Twelve Days of Christmas' again without thinking of all these curious connections! In a way, sad connections! It's sad that a bird as amiable and winsome as a partridge had such libidinous symbolism!"

Melanie: "What's libidinous?"

Babička: "I think the children have heard enough about libido for one evening. Why don't we take turns reading Dickens's *Christmas Carol*?"

But Babička herself was not exactly happy about the curious connections her curiosity had discovered, and on Epiphany Day, the day before she was flying back to California, she suddenly asked, "Has Pulu been blessed?"

"What do you mean—blessed?" asked Alison.

"Blessed by a priest."

"The Catholic church encourages the use of blessings," said Philip. "It has ceremonies for blessing persons, places, and things. When I got my first bike, Mother and Father took me and the bike to the church, and the priest prayed that the Lord Jesus would protect the child who rode that bike."

"I think that's beautiful!" said Alison wonderingly.

"Do priests bless animals and birds?" asked Melanie, visibly excited.

"Animals and birds and plants and seeds and ears and

61

throats and Christmas trees and everything God has created!"
said Babička. "Do you remember all the earaches you had when
you began going to kindergarten at St. Wenceslaus School,
Philip?"

"And you and Sister Miriam took me to the priest and had
him bless my ears!"

"Babička! Babička! Can we have Pulu blessed today? Will
you call the priest right now?" cried Melanie.

"I think it would be a blessed thing for Pulu and all of us to
have a private blessing service for him on the twelfth day of
Christmas."

"Maybe then I will be able to sing 'The Twelve Days of
Christmas' again without thinking of all those libidinous connections!" whispered Alison.

The priest was more than willing to conduct a private blessing service for Pulu.

"Animals and pets are usually blessed on October 4, the
Feast of St. Francis, but since that is long past I think Epiphany
Day is a good day to bless your chukar partridge. After all, the
Wise Men were from the East and very likely were well ac-
quainted with the red-legged partridge and may even have had
them as pets in their households."

"What a lovely thought!" said Alison.

Pulu seemed to want Babička to hold him through the brief
ceremony. They clustered in a half-circle around him while the
priest read Psalm 104. The priest's prayer was brief, as if to add
his words to that great hymn of praise and thanksgiving to the
Creator of all creation would be unfitting.

"Father, we ask your blessing on this partridge, in the
name of Jesus our Lord, Amen."

Everyone at breakfast the next morning was quiet and sad,
for Babička was leaving on a ten o'clock plane. Her bags were

neatly packed and resting open on the bed for the things to be tucked in at the last minute, such as her brush and comb and toothbrush. It was a hearty breakfast, meant to keep Babička's energy up all the way to California, but everyone just pecked at it listlessly. Even Pulu lost interest after eating a few pieces of his favorite sausage and hopped down from his plate and left the room.

"I think," said Philip, looking at his watch, "that we had better get your bags into the car and begin to think of leaving."

"I'll go shut my bags and check my purse for the umpteenth time for tickets, money, and keys," said Babička.

The twins were clearing the table when she returned and stared at them with a puzzled, almost irritated look.

"I enjoy being teased as much as I enjoy teasing, but not when it goes too far."

Alison and Philip paused on their way out of the room.

"What's the matter, Babička?" asked Michael and Melanie together.

"And I especially dislike it when the teasers who have gone too far pretend innocence!"

Babička's eyes were really snapping now.

"Have you kids done something?" asked Alison.

"Come and see!"

They followed Babička to the guest room, where her bags still rested on the bed, but the neatly folded top layers of things were scattered all over the bed and floor.

"I don't think this is one bit funny, and I must say I'm extremely surprised that you two would do such a thing!"

"Melanie and Michael, I'm horrified!" exclaimed Alison.

"This isn't mischief. This borders on—vandalism!" said Philip harshly.

"But we didn't do it!" cried Melanie. "Unless—unless you

63

did it, Michael!"

"Goll—lee—ee!" exclaimed Michael. "I'm disgusted that you all think I would do such a thing!"

They stood looking helplessly at the scattered articles of clothing.

"Where's Pulu?" Philip suddenly asked.

"Pulu! Of course, it was Pulu!" cried Michael.

"But Pulu is not mean! And Pulu loves Babička!"

Alison stopped suddenly. "That's it! That's just it! Pulu figured out in her tiny little bird brain that Babička is leaving today. She hoped that if she dumped things out of her bag, maybe she wouldn't go!"

"Oh, that precious bird!" whispered Babička, tears streaming down her face. "Find him! Oh, please find him!"

Michael found him under his plaid jacket, which he had neglected to hang up yesterday—found him only because he saw the jacket moving back into the dark corner of the closet. He brought him to Babička, who cuddled him close to her wet cheek. Melanie reached out to trace gently the broad black band that framed his creamy cheek and throat.

"Pulu, you silly, silly bird!"

"Melanie," said Philip thoughtfully, "you speak more truly than you know. Pulu is indeed a silly bird. The word 'silly' comes from an Anglo-Saxon word, 'seely,' which means— you'd never guess it! It means blessed!"

In the Bahamas

Babička's departure was the hardest for Pulu to bear. Melanie and Michael went back to school, which for them was not the dull-dull experience it is for most kids their age. By this time they had caught on that not even boring teachers can kill the fun of learning. Philip returned to his feasting on words in his carrel in the university library, and Alison to her counseling mixed-up kids in the elementary school. Once again Pulu was placed in his security cell five days a week, and once again he began playing his hide-and-seek game immediately after breakfast.

For Pulu the rest of January was more or less a bore, until life around him erupted into a fever of hurrying and scurrying that involved numerous telephone calls and much searching of drawers and closets for swimming suits, shorts, sandals, sunglasses, and suntan lotion. It all started rather suddenly when Philip came home one day and announced that if they all so willed it they were flying to the Bahamas in two days for two weeks in a hotel apartment on the beach. Two weeks of swimming in the clearest water in the world. Two weeks of sunning on the purest sand on earth. Miles and miles of it. Plus exploring wrecks and caves and rocks and the original Treasure Island. Snorkeling. Playing with incredibly intelligent gentle dolphins. Cruising on a glassbottom boat and seeing the fantastic undersea world of the Bahamas.

"Exciting restaurants! Superb cuisine! Exotic seafoods! Philip, Philip, you've done it again. You've succumbed to a persuasive travel agent!" laughed Alison. "Was she travel-poster pretty?"

"Wrong again, my dear skeptic! Perry was all booked to go to the Bahamas with his family but last night his father suddenly became so ill he had to be taken to the hospital by ambulance. Sad to say it's terminal—and soon. So it was either cancel his reservation or let us have it for the same reasonable rate. Very reasonable! No changes necessary. Our family fits Perry's, you know—two adults, two kids."

"Pulu! Don't forget Pulu!" cried the twins.

"Sorry, Pulu! I guess I did forget you," said Philip. "But he can stay with Grandpa and Bestemor."

"Who are flying to Arizona tomorrow to visit my Aunt Kari. Sorry, I forgot to tell you," said Alison. "Aside from Pulu, I think everything can be arranged. I've accumulated lots of sick leave days. It sounds great, Philip. Just the time to flee Midwest winter. I've never been able to figure out why the cold gets stronger as the days get longer."

By bedtime the next night everything was arranged save for Pulu. The twins' teacher agreed to their absence if they would make an hour report to the class on the history, geography, archeology, and culture of the Bahamas.

68

"I'll report on the pirates," said Michael. "Melanie can do the other stuff."

"What about Pulu?" asked Melanie.

"Perry called the owner of the Lime Hill Hotel, and they said it was OK to bring a pet partridge. He suggested that we call the Ministry of Agriculture and Fisheries for an import permit for Pulu. I did that, and they said they would send some forms for us to fill out. We have to apply in writing."

"But we're leaving tomorrow!" wailed Alison and the twins in dismay.

"I know! I know! I have to admit I'm nonplused."

"I won't go without Pulu," said Melanie flatly. "The rest of you can go and I'll stay home with Pulu."

"Don't be silly!" said Philip.

"I gotta great idea!" exploded Michael. "We'll smuggle Pulu in! In Current Events this morning one of the kids reported that a Mafia drug trafficker was picked up by the Feds in Miami. He was smuggling drugs from Colombia through the Bahamas. Well, we'll smuggle Pulu *into* the Bahamas! We can carry him on board the plane in his basket."

"It just might work!" mused Philip. "Pulu is used to being carried along with us in his basket. What's the longest he's had to stay in it?"

"The time we took him to the Wisconsin-Minnesota football game and didn't dare let him out because of the crowds. It was about four hours in all."

"A nonstop flight from Chicago to the Bahamas is about four hours. It just might work, but the Malecha family had better sit down right now and plan the strategy. We're far from pros in the smuggling business."

"Not as amateur as you think, Daddy!" said Alison tartly. "A lot of cookies have been smuggled out of this house by a cunning clique in this very neighborhood."

It was decided that the twins should rise early the next

69

morning and take a long bike ride around Lake Wingra. A swift one, making it necessary for Pulu to run, flutter, and fly to keep up. After an extra-big breakfast of his favorite foods he would be more than ready for a nap in his familiar basket. Alison would carry the basket when they boarded the plane at O'Hare.

"Mother has the most innocent face and is the logical one of us to carry a capacious Mexican basket."

"The X-ray machine!" whispered Alison. "We are forgetting that all carry-on baggage has to go through the X-ray machine!"

"So we are!" said Philip glumly.

"Will the X-ray machine kill Pulu?" asked Melanie anxiously.

Philip: "Not any more than X-rays kill human beings. Airports use X-ray machines to look for dangerous weapons like guns, knives, bombs, et cetera. They reveal the shapes of things in hand baggage."

Michael: "But Pulu isn't shaped like a gun or knife! When Pulu is sleeping he looks like a football."

Melanie: "Or a round loaf of Bestemor's brown bread."

Alison: "The kids are right! The X-ray machine doesn't picture things clearly. Pulu could look like any one of the strange things we women carry in our oversize purses and baskets."

Philip: "Like the frozen venison roast your sister in Duluth brought in her handbag, and it began to defrost before she got to Madison. It just might work! Pulu tucked up in sleep won't look any more suspicious than a loaf of bread. Besides, who is going to suspect a lovely woman with such a handsome husband and beautiful children of being a terrorist?"

It was decided that Alison was to sit as far toward the front as she could, while the others were to sit in rear seats lest Pulu hear their voices and clamor to get out of his basket. Philip was to ask if his wife could be assigned a seat next to empty seats.

70

Everything went according to plan.

"My wife is not feeling very well this morning," Philip said, and the stewardess gave her a window seat with two empty seats beside her, for the plane was only half full. But just before the plane took off, a florid portly woman sitting alone across the aisle from Alison decided to move into the seat next to her.

"It looks like we're two women traveling alone. We might as well keep each other company," she said as she struggled to push her considerable carry-on baggage under both the aisle and middle seats.

Alison quickly opened one of the books Philip had taken out of the library to bring along, *The Ephemeral Islands: A Natural History of the Bahamas,* by David G. Campbell. If she spoke, Pulu in his basket at her feet would hear her voice and begin chukar-chattering.

"I'm staying at the Royal Bahamian Hotel. Where are you staying?"

Alison turned a page and said nothing.

"Hmm! Are you deaf or something?"

Alison said nothing. The woman angrily snapped her seat-belt.

"You just can't tell by looks anymore! Even the pretty and nicely dressed ones are rude. Or uppity!"

She settled down into hostile silence. Alison, miserable over her forced rudeness, read about the Bahamian woodstar hummingbird, "the living flame" that could beat its wings two hundred times a second, and fervently prayed that Bird Pulu would remain practically comatose in his basket until they had cleared customs. But when the stewardess passed the snacks she knew their wild and impulsive chance-taking was doomed. Pulu loved nuts and he could smell them a mile away. If only her seatmate would not open her packet! But she did, of course,

71

with much fuming and fussing about the way things were sealed up these days. When she began noisily munching and crunching, Pulu stirred in his basket.

"What do you have in that basket?"

Alison turned a page and read about the plump-bodied bottle spider, otherwise known as the black widow spider, perhaps "the most venomous animal in the Islands." Pulu chucked a low inquiring chuck.

"I knew it! I knew it! I knew you had something you shouldn't have in that basket! Stewardess! Stewardess!"

There will soon be something more venomous than a black widow spider on the islands, thought Alison. A plump-bodied white widow-tourist!

"This woman has a chicken or a bird in that basket," the woman told the stewardess.

The stewardess's brown eyes surveyed the accuser and the accused coolly, then twinkled with laughter.

"Really? May I see it, please?"

Alison lifted the cover and Pulu stepped out, perched on Alison's wrist and stretched his neck and wings—to uncramp them, of course—but meanwhile he exhibited his lovely creamy neck and the distinctive black bars on his tawny flanks.

"See! I told you she was carrying something forbidden!"

"What a beautiful bird!" exclaimed the stewardess. "May I show him to the pilots?"

Pulu transferred willingly to the stewardess's wrist. She started for the cockpit but turned back for a moment to say, with vinegar in her voice: "Passengers are permitted to carry on manageable pets in cages or baskets that can be stored under the seats."

With the lid blown off the plot, so to speak—or at least off the basket—Alison and Pulu joined the rest of the family in the rear of the plane. After dinner was served (the stewardess

72

brought several packets of honey roasted peanuts for Pulu) the twins proudly went up and down the aisle showing Pulu to the passengers and answering all their inquisitive questions. Alison's former seatmate coldly turned her back when they walked by.

"We are a bit anxious about getting Pulu through customs without an entry permit," Philip told the stewardess as they neared Nassau.

"No problem," she said. "You will be the last to leave the plane. Carry Pulu in the basket. Take the Nothing to Declare line, and I'm positive they will just wave you through. If you have any trouble, just let me know. One of the customs guys is engaged to my best friend. He knows how to wink at no-account things."

But there were no hitches or snags the rest of the day. None whatever. The plane landed on schedule at the Nassau International Airport. The owner of the Lime Hill Hotel and Apartments met them with his minibus, stopped at a supermarket (disappointingly like the ones at home) so that they could stock up on groceries, and took them to his hotel on Coral Harbour. He introduced them to another passenger in the minibus.

"Dis Sam Palmer. He back with us for da fifth winter."

"You were on our plane!" said Michael.

"Or you were on *my* plane. Sure, I saw the whole drama with your partridge."

"Do you come for sailing or snorkeling or both?" asked Philip.

"Neither. Nor for shelling or drug-trafficking or nightclubbing or gambling or golfing or deep sea fishing. I came to do nothing. Absolutely nothing. Unless you call reading murder mysteries and lying in the sun doing something. And smoking two packs of cigarettes a day. It's getting so one can't even do that in the states any more."

73

Alison exclaimed with delight at the trees, flowers, and bushes they passed.

"Hibiscus! Orchids! Tulip trees! Poinsettias! All growing wild alongside the road!"

"Look at that big patch of mother-in-law tongues!" said Philip. "You threw out our plant, remember?"

"I hate the name! My mother-in-law is a perfect dear."

"*My* mother-in-law is nicer than yours!" sang Philip.

"Please, Daddy!" pleaded Melanie. "Don't play that silly old mother-in-law game with Mom on our vacation!"

The apartment was tiny but adequate. The beach was wide and excellent, the sea blue-green and infinite. The breeze blowing through the screens was June-in-Wisconsin benign. A bird never heard in Wisconsin perched on a branch of a tree on the patio and sang loudly and longly—seemingly without repeating itself.

"Can it be—? Is it—oh, I hope, I hope!—is it a mockingbird?" asked Alison.

"A Bahamian mockingbird. It don't mock other birds. Sings its own melody," said the landlord.

"Speaking of birds," said Philip, "while Mother and I settle in I suggest that you kids get into your swimsuits and take Pulu to the beach. He deserves some sand-fun after being scrunched in that basket for hours."

"Are there sharks out there?" Melanie asked the landlord fearfully.

"You see dat crazy movie, too, chile? You know dat dey makin' de next one on de island right now? Jaws 3 or 4. I lose count. We Bahamians don't like nobody scarin' de tourists. No, chile, you ain't be eat by shark out der. I born der in Coral Harbour an' I ne'er hear nobody be bit up by shark. De mos' fright'ning ting you see on de beach is sand crabs, and all dey want to do is get out of you way and hide. You see lizards on de

74

rock walls on de patio. We like dem. Dey eat de mosquitoes. You partridge, he have plenty fun tryin' to catch dem."

Sam Palmer was standing in his doorway smoking a cigarette when Melanie and Michael came out in their swimming suits.

"From the sound of it, you kids have the bedroom on the other side of the wall from me. It's pretty thin, and I hope I won't have to listen to the horrible music teenagers are addicted to. But you are preteens, so maybe your taste in music hasn't been polluted yet."

"We didn't bring a radio or tape recorder," said Michael stiffly, but didn't tell him that their parents didn't allow them on vacations. But he could not resist saying, "We hope that we won't have to inhale your cigarette smoke. Our mom is very allergic to it."

"Even Steven!" grinned Sam. "I like your spunk! I'll be careful."

Never in Pulu's short life had he experienced a sandy beach such as the Lime Hill Beach. Nor was there in his chukar partridge subconscious a seashore of pure white sand like this coralline sand constantly washed and moved about by the waves and tides. The sand was clean, loose, and perfect for dusting. He ignored the waves of blue-green water advancing in swells, pushing foam fingers as far as they could thrust them, and retreating again. The twins jumped on the incoming swells as onto a horse and rode them in, squealing with delight. But Pulu, true to his instincts, flipped sand swells up and over his back and chuck-chuckled with delight.

"Hey, mon! I tell you dat bird sure crazy 'bout sand!" marveled the landlord, who had wandered down to see how the American kids and their bird liked his beach.

"Why does the landlord talk like that?" Michael asked Sam Palmer later when the latter came down to stretch out in a beach

75

chair to smoke and read. "Didn't he go to school? Don't they teach grammar in the Bahamian schools?"

"Kid," said Sam, "Jim can talk the Queen's English better than any Englishman on the island. But like any true Bahamian he proudly speaks the Bahamian dialect. I myself think it is a lovely and colorful way of talking. If you ask Jim why he talks Bahamian he'll say, 'I was born and grow wit' dialect. Who don' like der way I soun' can lump it.' "

When the family explored farther reaches and beaches eastward the next day, Pulu discovered the holes and crevices that honeycombed the porous limestone rock and promptly acted as if he had found a lost chukar partridge paradise. At first they were alarmed by his sudden disappearances, but soon they were hilariously playing the "Find Pulu" game.

The next day they took a bus to Nassau and explored the city and the harbor. Alison was impressed with the aristocratic features and natural elegance of the Bahamian women.

"They all look as if they stepped off the cover of Vogue magazine!"

The Bahamians, in turn, were impressed with Pulu, who trotted close behind the family or rode on a shoulder of his choosing if there were too many feet on the street.

"Hey, mon! Dat some bird der!"

One elderly man stopped them to discuss chukar partridges. He turned out to be a Bahamian who preferred to speak classy cultured English to foreigners.

"The chukar partridge was introduced to the Bahamas. It is not a native bird. The only one that survived on this island died of old age in the aviary at Ardastra Gardens. There are some on Eleuthera, I am told."

"I regret that we won't have time to get over to Eleuthera," said Philip, "although it may be the only chance for Pulu ever to see his own kith and kin."

The next day, after swimming to their bodies' content, Michael and Melanie asked if they could explore the beach to the westward with Pulu. Alison and Philip were stretched out on beach chairs chatting about books and writing with Sam Palmer, who wrote mysteries as well as read them. When he assured them that there were no hazards other than sand fleas, the twins were allowed to go alone. However, when they had not returned in two hours Alison and Philip became anxious and went looking for them. When they had not found them after wading and walking a mile, they became genuinely worried and wondered if they should call the police—or someone.

"I suppose 911 doesn't operate here in the Bahamas," said Philip, "but there has to be someone to call in emergencies. Shall we go in here and ask if we can use the telephone?"

A dog leaped up on a garden wall, barked furiously at them, and was joined by two other dogs in the garden.

"I guess not!" said Philip.

Just then the garden gate burst open and exploded a tangle of dogs and kids, and the kids turned out to be Michael and Melanie. They were followed by a slim dark woman and a handsome blonde young man. Pulu sat calmly on the young man's shoulder.

"Mommy! Daddy! We found new friends!"

"They're from Minnesota!"

"They've got three dogs!"

"Pulu has already made friends with all of them—Susie and Sally and Sophie and Anne Marie and Ted."

The barking dogs and shouting twins leaped in a circle around Alison and Philip, who reached out their hands to the young couple.

"I assume you are Ted, but are you Sally or Susie or Anne Marie or Sophie?" asked Philip.

"She's Anne Marie!" shrieked the twins.

Philip: "How do you say 'Calm down!' in Bahamese?"

Ted: "The kids in the school where I teach say 'Chill out!' "

Philip: "Okay, you kids and dogs, chill out!"

Ted: "Our dogs are Bahamian potcake dogs—that means mongrel—but they understand Minnesota English better than Bahamian dialect. PIPE DOWN! SHUT UP!"

"We were worried when Michael and Melanie and Pulu didn't return," said Alison.

"We're sorry we kept them so long," said Anne Marie, "but it took a while for everyone to get over the excitement of the dogs chasing Pulu up the bluff. I was out walking with the dogs, and when they saw a partridge—well, you can imagine that things got pretty lively for a while. But they're all friends now. Won't you come in?"

"Please! Please!" begged the twins.

Melanie: "Anne Marie has chocolate chip cookies!"

Michael: "Ted cracked two coconuts we picked up in his yard and made a yummy cold drink from the coconut milk."

Melanie: "Anne Marie is making fudge. It's cooling down, and we're going to take turns beating it."

"My mother was just down to see us and brought all these goodies," explained Anne Marie.

Philip: "We'd love to come in, but it might not be wise. My wife is allergic to dogs."

Melanie: "But they don't come in the house, Daddy!

Ted: "They stay on the porch. Our landlady won't permit dogs in the house."

It was ten o'clock at night before Ted brought them back to their Lime Hill apartment. Sam Palmer stood in the doorway, his cigarette glowing in the dark.

"We dun reach," said Philip, who had been learning some Bahamian phrases from Ted and remembered how to say, "We have arrived."

"It's about time," said Sam. "I was just about to send a search party for you."

During the rest of their vacation their new friends were chauffeurs, tour guides, sports partners, chefs. Anne Marie was free to take them in her battered Datsun wagon to all the sites and attractions on the island. To Alison's delight she seemed to know the names of all the flora and fauna and could teach them to recognize the Casuarina with its drooping, feathery branches and the sea grape with its smooth, leathery leaves with prominent shiny reddish veins. She was also a history nut and dropped exciting little nuggets easily and casually into their conversation.

"The sea grape is the first plant Columbus saw."

"The British architect whom the Benedictines engaged to design St. Augustine's Monastery gave up his career and himself became a monk."

Ted was a sports nut. On Saturday, after watching him coach a junior high school bowling team, they watched his team (on which he was the only white person) win a softball game. On the beach in front of his house he invented the "Pass the Partridge" game when he noticed that Pulu, folded together for carrying, resembled a football. Pulu quickly learned the game and as he accommodated to it the passes became longer and the hilarity stronger. Until the game ended in a wild dash into the surf and a swim out to the breakers, Pulu was more football than partridge. But as they frolicked in the water he resumed his true chukar partridge identity and dusted in the sand.

On Sunday night occurred the event that made Pulu a hero on the island and put his picture on the front page of the daily paper. The family returned late, very late, from a brimful day on the beaches of Paradise Island and a night dining on Ted and Anne Marie's crazily mixed-up Bahamian and Minnesotan cuisine. For example, conch pizza! Colby cheese and okra omelet!

The twins were so tired that they did not even brush their teeth before they went to bed. The parents knew it but were too tired to care. Within half an hour everyone was so sound asleep that firecrackers exploding under their beds would not have awakened them. Pulu, who graciously divided his nights between the parents' and the twins' bedrooms, chose this night to sleep on Michael's pillow. He snuggled against the flimsy wall that formed the partition between Sam Palmer's bedroom and the twins' and closed his eyes. But sound sleep did not come to Pulu. He opened his eyes, stirred restlessly. Closed them again. Relaxed and leaned against the wall. The wall was warm and becoming warmer! He opened his eyes again and became partridge-alert. In a matter of seconds the wall became hot!

Pulu's partridge brain somehow knew that it would be impossible to arouse Michael, so he flew screaming chukar alarm sounds to Philip's bed and pecked his bare shoulder savagely. So savagely that Philip leaped to his feet and lunged at him.

"Pulu, have you gone crazy?"

But he instantly smelled the smoke that by this time was pouring through a hole in the charred wall and saw the flame traveling up the wall behind the twins' beds.

The rest was a wild uproar of shouting, screaming, running, pounding on doors. The twins were pulled out of their beds. Sam Palmer, drugged with smoke and his right arm singed with third degree burns, was rescued from the bed where he had fallen asleep reading a murder mystery and smoking. His hand, holding a lighted cigarette, had sagged to the floor beside the wine bottle and had ignited the shag rug to a slow smoldering fire that eventually reached the wall.

By the time the fire department arrived, the landlord and Philip and the other hotel guests had the fire pretty much under control. After the ambulance carried Sam Palmer—groggy but conscious enough to be horribly remorseful—off to the hospital, everyone stood around to examine the bloody stab wounds on Philip's shoulder and to extol Pulu.

"I tell you dat some of us would be fryin' in hell now if it hadna bin for dat bird!" said the landlord.

He immediately granted Pulu and the Malecha family the freedom of the Bahamas and of the Lime Hill Hotel for their lifetime.

The story of course made the papers. A small crowd, including several reporters and photographers, was at the airport to see them off. The customs officials winked at Pulu's illegal entry. The same stewardess was on their plane. But, fortunately, not the malicious, venomous white widow-tourist!

Sam Palmer, his right arm bandaged and in a sling, was the last one to say goodbye. And the last words he said to them were: "I want you to know that I have quit smoking forever."

"Forever?" asked Michael.

"Forever and ever, so help me God!"

Pulu Did It!

Needless to say, after all that fun in the sun and the sand, after all that excitement, after all that hero worship, coming back home again to the confinement of a security cage five days a week was not exactly Pulu's bowl of cashews. He did not greet his liberator, the first one home from school, with the same spontaneous joy as previously.

"He's not only dopey, he's mopey!" said Melanie, unaware that even she was now calling Pulu "he."

"Maybe he is entering partridge adolescence," said Alison, who also had switched genders for Pulu without realizing it. "Adolescence sometimes produces some strange changes in temperament."

"Maybe Pulu is even beyond adolescence and is pining for a beautiful female. Let's hope that the priest's blessing chased out only the inordinate wicked lust a chukar partridge was thought to have and left him with a partridge's ordinate proclivity," said Philip.

"Cut it out, Dad!" snapped Michael. "You don't have to impress us with your big words."

"Daddy is just talking about Pulu's sex life," said Alison. "Which I must confess I'm beginning to worry about. With no other chukar partridge around, is Pulu doomed to a mateless life? Do you suppose he could mate with a grouse or a prairie chicken?"

"Or a pheasant?"

"Or a bobwhite?"

"Or a wild turkey?"

"Or a great horned owl?"

"Now you're all getting silly!" said Philip. "But let's face it. We have a problem."

"It's Pulu's problem," said Michael, matter-of-factly.

"Meanie!" cried Melanie. "Pulu's problem is all of us's problem!"

Both Easter and spring are moveable feasts, so to speak. This year Easter moved to its latest and spring to its earliest. By the first of March there were catkins on the hazel and aspen in the Wingra woods. Buds had swelled to bursting in the thickets. Thin Vs of wild geese flew high in the sky on their way home to Canada.

The weather was so springlike that after church one Sunday the twins and Pulu went for a bike ride around the lake. They came back springful of news. Or newsful of spring.

"We saw robins!"

"And red-wing blackbirds!"

"Uff!" exclaimed Alison. "It's too soon! What if we get a sudden blast of winter?"

"Where's Pulu?" asked Philip. "Didn't he go with you?"

84

"Yes, but he disappeared into Redwing Marsh."

"Don't worry, he'll come back. Remember, Pulu is adolescent—and it's spring—and adolescents like to be outside in the spring."

"Pulu is beyond adolescence, and he's yearning for a mate," said Alison sadly. "Oh, Philip, I feel so guilty about him! We've selfishly cared only about ourselves, about having Pulu as our pet. We haven't cared about Pulu and his natural instincts and urges at all!"

"I admit being a man or a buck or a bull or a tom or a cock isn't always so easy. Come to think of it, I have to admit that although I call Pulu 'he' I actually have thought of him as sexless, neither male nor female, just a gray neuter. Maybe it's because the Creator saw fit to make the male and female chukar partridge almost indistinguishable. I wonder why. He sure equipped the male prairie chicken with a lot of flamboyant foppery to display during courtship."

Pulu returned, of course, and on Monday, when Philip stayed in bed all day and read books because of a sore throat, Pulu practically never left his side.

"What a compassionate male Pulu is!" said Philip when the others had returned home. "Women are supposed to have it all over us men when it comes to tenderheartedness. But neither you, Alison, nor you, Melanie, offered to sit at my bedside all day and hold my hand. Ergo, this male bird is more tenderhearted than you females."

Alison hung her coat in the closet, pulled a chair beside the bed, sat down, and reached for Philip's hand.

"Dearest darling, forgive me! Allow me to make up for my hardheartedness! I had planned to brew you your favorite tea, squeeze a pitcher of fresh orange juice, and make a light supper of chicken breasts and snow peas. But I'll put the chicken and snow peas I brought home in the refrig and sit here with you and hold your hand. Melanie and Michael can bring us a Coke and heat up a can of pork and beans for supper. Or we could have weiners and potato chips. I'll tenderly feed you chips with my own hand. Chip by chip by chip by chip."

Philip pinched her—and not at all tenderly.

"Out of my sight, woman! To the kitchen with you!"

A half hour later a loud shout from the bedroom brought all three of them out of the kitchen to Philip's bedside. He was staring dumbfounded at Alison's side of the bed where Pulu had been sitting. He was staring at an egg!

"He—he—she—Pulu did it!"

They all looked in amazement at the yellow-white spotted egg. They could not believe it but had to believe it. After all, an egg is an egg, and no male has ever laid an egg. They looked from the egg to Pulu, who had suddenly, clearly, and unmistakably made a statement about—herself! Pulu had finally identified herself as being other than they had thought her to be. Pulu herself did not seem at all surprised at what she had just done.

Suddenly Alison and Melanie remembered simultaneously the song they had sung when they had been quarreling with Philip and Michael about whether Pulu was a cock or a hen. They grabbed each other's hands and danced around the bedroom.

Ha—Ha—Ha—HAHA!
Ha—Ha—Ha—HAHA!
Pulu's not a cock!
Pulu is a HEN—N—N!

Michael ignored the gloat-song, picked Pulu up in his arms, and stroked her.

"Can we keep calling—" he visibly gulped— "her—Pulu?"

"How about Polly?" asked Melanie.

"Fully female though she be," said Philip, "I think we'll have to keep calling her Pulu. Think how confusing it would be, Michael, if I started calling you Millie after calling you Michael ever since you were born."

"It's going to be hard enough just to change all the pronouns and our very thought patterns!" laughed Alison. "It will be almost as hard as churches having to change the sexist language of the Bible, the liturgy, and the hymns."

They telephoned Bestemor and Grandpa and told them the amazing news.

"I always thought he was a she," said Grandpa. "He was too much like a she to be a he."

"He means not strutty and cocky enough to be a cock," said Bestemor.

Babička sighed a very audible sigh of relief when they called to tell her the stunning news. "Praise the Lord! Now I can use all the adjectives for Pulu I couldn't use when I thought she was a he. You just don't call males bonny, adorable, pretty, beautiful. Or pulchritudinous. Pulchritudinous Pulu. Doesn't that sound great? I think I shall have to write a poem about pulchritudinous Pulu."

Pulu continued to make her statements, one each day. They found them here, there, and everywhere around the house. Under chairs and couches, among the plants in the mini-arb, in wastebaskets, the mitten and glove basket, in drawers the twins carelessly left open before they left for school. It became a game to find Pulu's daily egg. When there were a dozen buffy spotted eggs in the refrig, Philip suggested that they have a Pulu-egg omelet for breakfast the next day. The twins were horrified.

Michael: "I'd feel like a cannibal!"

Melanie: "I'd feel like a murderer!"

Not until Babička straightened them out in a telephone call would the twins eat Pulu's statements.

"What's this I hear about you two refusing to eat Pulu's eggs? Pulu's gifts to you? Well, well! I was planning to send you a box of chocolates, but if you are refusing to accept and eat Pulu's gifts to you, maybe you won't accept and eat mine!"

For several weeks they had a Pulu-egg omelet for Sunday breakfast. But when spring finally settled down to stay and Pulu spent most of her time outdoors, they no longer found eggs in the house.

"Obviously she's making a nest," said Philip.

"Poor thing," sighed Alison. "She wants to be a mother but doesn't know that her eggs are infertile."

Pulu continued to lay her eggs in some hidden nest, but as yet she had not begun to sit on them. For the present her mating impulse seemed to be as strong as her nesting impulse. One afternoon she heard the ruffed grouse drumming in Wingra Marsh and rushed off to find the drummers. She was gone so long that they feared they would never see her again. Eventually she did return, but slowly, reluctantly, and dejectedly.

"Poor Pulu," said Melanie sadly. "Didn't they like you?"

"Pulu, Pulu!" said Alison. "You want to find a lover, you want to be a mother, and you've been rejected."

Strangely enough, when a ruffed grouse male did appear one day and courted her, displaying all his beautiful plumage, Pulu was completely uninterested.

"He must not be going about it the right way, the chukar partridge way," said Philip.

When Pulu began to be absent all day and all night they knew that she had decided that she had enough eggs for a family and had begun to brood. It was futile to put out food for her because the squirrels and chipmunks ate it before she came to get it. When she did come, they fed her, watched her eat, and held her until she squirmed to get back to her nest.

"I miss her so!" mourned Melanie, after Pulu had been

absent for almost a week. "Do you suppose she'll sit on those eggs forever?"

"How long would it take for the eggs to hatch if they were fertile?" asked Michael.

"The incubation period for chukar partridges is twenty-four days," said Philip.

"I'm worried that Pulu might suffer a personality change from her disappointment over not having babies and become a nervous, maladjusted bird," said Alison.

"I don't s'pose there's such a thing as a psychiatrist for partridges," said Michael.

"If you think that's funny, Michael Malecha, then you need a psychiatrist yourself!" snapped Melanie, close to tears.

Pulu returned that evening but stayed no longer than half an hour. The twins tried to follow her, but her instinct to conceal her nest made her too clever for them. Every night after school the next week they searched the twenty miles of roads and lanes in the Arb, but since Philip forbade them to step off the trails they had no luck.

"Golly, Dad, can't we go off the path a couple feet if we think Pulu's nest is close by?"

"Not one step! There are hundreds of species of plants growing in the Arb. It's peak time for wild flowers. Hepatica, bloodroot, pasque flowers, marsh marigolds. To step on one plant and destroy it is a crime against the whole wonderful attempt to build this arboretum and to restore and preserve the native Wisconsin ecological communities."

On Friday night, when Philip and Alison were at a banquet at the university, Michael and Melanie called Babička collect, as she always urged them to do if they had any problems.

"Well!" she exclaimed after they had explained the situation. "You *do* have a problem! Poor Pulu! She will sit on those eggs until the snow flies if something isn't done. What you have

89

to do, of course, is switch the infertile eggs for fertile chicken eggs without Pulu knowing it. I heard of a man in Rochester, Minnesota—the wild goose city, you know—who had a pet wild goose sitting on infertile eggs. About the time the eggs should have incubated, the man whisked away the rotten eggs and replaced them with fluffy day-old goslings he had bought. The wild goose never realized the switch. If you could get some fertile hen's eggs—"

"Yes, but Babička, we can't switch the eggs if we can't find Pulu's nest!"

"Well, find it then! Obviously you've been looking in the wrong places. Get the Audubon bird guide and read to me what it says about the nesting habits of chukar partridges."

Melanie found the bird guide quickly, and the chukar partridge page was already marked.

"It says '8–15 buffy brown-spotted eggs in a grass- and feather-lined scrape in the shelter of rocks or bushes.' "

" 'A scrape in the shelter of rocks,' " repeated Babička. "Chukar partridges are birds of mountain slopes. A scrape is a fault in a surface of rock. I'll just bet you kids have been looking for Pulu's nest in woods and swamps and wetlands! Are there any dry and stony areas nearby?"

"Our patio," chuckled Michael.

"Patios!" exclaimed Babička. "Patios have pebbles or cobblestones or flagstones or gravel. Patios have outdoor fireplaces, some of them pretty elaborate stone or brick fireplaces. Some of them are well concealed from the street, even from the house. Wisconsin isn't California, and patios in Wisconsin are pretty much abandoned for nine months of the year. They can be pretty lonesome, solitary, private places, just the kind of a place a broody chukar partridge is looking for! I'll just bet you kids will find Pulu's nest right nearby in some neighbor's backyard!"

And so they did! Three houses away, no farther than a city

block from their own house, Pulu was sitting on a dozen "buffy brown-spotted eggs" in the ashes of an old fireplace in a very sheltered patio.

Pulu seemed almost pleased to be discovered.

"Don't worry, Pulu, honey," whispered Melanie. "We won't touch your eggs."

"Don't tell Pulu lies!" hissed Michael. "That's just what we're going to do as soon as she leaves her nest long enough for us to switch her eggs."

"Switch them with what? Where are we going to get fertile eggs?"

"From Tom's grandpa!"

"The one who gives Tom live chicks for his boa constrictor?"

"Yep! That's who! He'll give us some eggs just about ready to hatch, and we'll switch them with Pulu's eggs."

Melanie was so delighted with the plot Michael had hatched that she could not help herself and gave him an ecstatic hug. "Let's make this our secret! Let's not tell Mom and Dad about it until it's happened!"

Tom and his grandfather with the hatchery were so intrigued with the plot that they even offered to bring the eggs themselves the minute the twins called and said the coast was clear and Pulu had left the nest for a brief time.

"Park a block away from our house so Mom and Dad don't see what we're doing," warned Michael.

The twins took turns spying on Pulu. Two days later they called Tom's grandfather from the phone in the basement. Everything went smoothly according to plan. The switch was made. The human conspirators vanished from the scene but spied from the next yard to satisfy themselves that Pulu returned before the eggs had time to cool and that she suspected nothing.

91

"How long before the eggs hatch?" whispered Michael.

"Maybe a day. Could be two."

Because their class went on an all-day, last-week-of-school outing the next day, the twins did not come home until five o'clock and had no time to check on Pulu. Then, too, Bestemor and Grandpa had come with all the fixings for a picnic supper, and who could remember a partridge sitting on her eggs in another backyard when in one's own backyard one was sitting down to Bestemor's fried chicken, potato salad, fruit salad, butterhorns, and rhubarb torte?

Grandpa saw Pulu first when she came marching across the lawn followed by a scattering of fluffballs frantically trying to keep up with her determined advance.

"Well, I'll be!" he exclaimed. Ten eyes followed his pointing fork.

"Pulu!" screamed the twins, scrambling up from the table, dropping on their knees, and scooping the chicks up in their hands.

Alison followed them, scooped Pulu up, and held her close. "Pulu, you came home! You brought your family home to us!"

"What I want to know," said Philip after the excitement had simmered down somewhat, "is how Pulu managed to hatch a family from infertile eggs!"

The four adults listened in amazement while the twins explained the ingenious plot they—or rather, Michael—had hatched.

"It was Michael's idea," said Melanie, looking at him fondly.

"Melanie was the one who saw Pulu leave the nest so we could make the switch," said Michael generously.

Philip, meanwhile, was surveying his family quietly. "I don't know who is prouder, Pulu of her family or Alison and I

92

of ours. All I can say, Alison, is that Pulu's eggs may have been infertile, but our children's imaginations for sure are not!"

"When you get done ogling that bird and those baby chicks," said Bestemor, "I wish you would all sit down and have seconds on this rhubarb torte before the meringue collapses!"

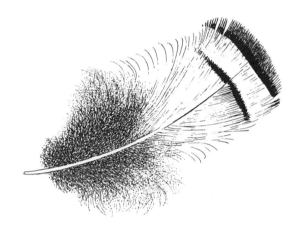